"It see[...]
to eac[...]

The light [...] [...]he palms fell [...] [...] face. His expression [...] no longer ironic or teasing. It reflected the same hunger Karen felt inside herself. She drew a deep breath.

"Nothing we can't cope with, I'm sure." She was pleased with the comparative steadiness of her voice. "Moonlight in Acapulco no doubt plays all sorts of tricks with our emotions. We needn't take it too seriously."

He held her away. "What are you afraid of, Karen?"

"I just told you." She managed a smile. "Moonlight in Acapulco. It goes to one's head."

It was ridiculous, strolling along in the moonlight discussing the possibility of making love as if talking about the weather, or was that the way that people behaved in his world?

MARJORIE LEWTY is a born romantic—and no wonder. Her father was a sailor and her mother worked in the theater. "It's all in the way you look at the world," she suggests. "Maybe if I hadn't been lucky enough to find love myself—in my parents, my husband, my children—I might have viewed the world with cynicism." As it is, she writes about "what is surely the most important and exciting part of growing up, and that is falling in love." She and her family live in Leamington, a pleasant town full of beautiful parks and old Georgian homes. "It is a good place for a writer to live and work," she says, "and here we hope and believe we may stay." They have two children.

Books by Marjorie Lewty

HARLEQUIN PRESENTS
140—THE FIRE IN THE DIAMOND
875—ACAPULCO MOONLIGHT

HARLEQUIN ROMANCE
2650—RIVIERA ROMANCE
2678—LOVERS' KNOT
2746—A LAKE IN KYOTO

These books may be available at your local bookseller.

Don't miss any of our special offers. Write to us at the following address for information on our newest releases.

Harlequin Reader Service
901 Fuhrmann Blvd.
P.O. Box 1325, Buffalo, NY 14269
Canadian address: P.O. Box 2800, Postal Station A,
5170 Yonge St., Willowdale, Ont. M2N 6J3

MARJORIE LEWTY

acapulco moonlight

Harlequin Books

TORONTO • NEW YORK • LONDON
AMSTERDAM • PARIS • SYDNEY • HAMBURG
STOCKHOLM • ATHENS • TOKYO • MILAN

Harlequin Presents first edition April 1986
ISBN 0-373-10875-3

Original hardcover edition published in 1985
by Mills & Boon Limited

Printed in U.S.A.

CHAPTER ONE

EVER since yesterday afternoon, when Ben broke the news to her, Karen had been feeling more and more worried, and by this morning, when she arrived at the factory and edged her Mini into the parking bay marked *Miss K. Lane*, the worry had changed to anger.

It wasn't fair, she fumed silently, slamming the car door and turning the key, Ben shouldn't be in danger of losing everything he had built up in his business over the last five years. She stood for a moment looking with affection at the low, neat factory building in the small industrial centre on the outskirts of the Midlands town, where she had worked with Ben Clark for three of those five years. She was almost as proud of the place as Ben himself was. As his secretary, and recently as his personal assistant, she had been involved in so many of the decisions that concerned the running of the factory and the comfort of the staff that she felt she had a personal stake in it all.

She pushed open the side door, stamping the slushy snow off her high-heeled black boots vigorously. *Damn* the bank manager! Couldn't he *see* what an utterly worthwhile man Ben was? Honest, hard-working, responsible, kind. A thoroughly *good* man. And a wizard in his own particular line, which was electronics. Heavens above, she grumbled to herself as she hung up her coat in the outer office, electronics was the up-and-coming thing, wasn't it? The communications industry that was going to transform all our lives. Surely a man as clever and inventive as

Ben Clark should be able to keep his firm viable, without being on the brink of disaster every other month?

Lucy, the young typist and odd-job-girl, came panting in just behind Karen, her cheeky face rosy from the keen January wind outside. 'Oh hello, Miss Lane, gosh, am I late? I had to wait ages for a bus. Brrh! What a brute of a morning. It's starting to snow again.' She wrenched off her mac and flung it over the back of the typing chair.

'Hadn't you'd better hang that up?' Karen suggested. 'We're on show this morning, remember?'

Lucy's hand flew to her mouth. 'Oh, golly, I forgot.' She hung the mac on the coat-rack next to Karen's red cord jacket and went over to uncover her typewriter, rubbing her hands together vigorously. 'What's so special about this important bod who's coming, anyway? Is he going to give Mr Clark a specially hefty order or something?'

'Something,' Karen said vaguely. There was no point, at this stage, in warning Lucy just how critical the visit of Mr Saul Marston, millionaire-tycoon, was likely to be. If he was interested in what he saw here Ben's troubles might be over. If not—well, Lucy would probably find herself out of a job at the end of the week. So would they all.

Karen smoothed down her scarlet pleated skirt and glanced in the mirror to check on her make-up and run a comb through her dark, shining hair. Except for evening dates she usually wore her hair down, curving into her neck, or tied back with a ribbon, but this morning she had arranged it in a knot on the top of her prettily-shaped head. A small detail, but today everything depended on giving this Saul Marston the impression of a well-run business, and Karen reckoned she looked like the competent business woman she felt herself to be. She just wished she didn't feel so churned up inside.

'Brew up some coffee, there's a dear,' she said to Lucy. 'I know it's early but we can do with it on a morning like this, and Mr Clark will be ready for some when he comes in.'

'Yes, Miss Lane, will do.' Lucy flashed an adoring smile towards Karen and scuttled away to the little cupboard-annexe where they kept the coffee machine.

'And you'd better have some more on for when Mr Marston arrives,' Karen called after her.

Lucy's pink face and frizzy gold head appeared round the cupboard door. 'What time's he coming?'

'Eleven.' Karen pushed open the door of the inner office that she shared with Ben. His car hadn't been in the car-park so he couldn't be here yet and she'd have time to tidy the place up before he arrived. They'd worked late last night, going over all the figures with a fine toothcomb, in readiness for this vital meeting this morning, and they had both been too tired to set the office to rights then.

But Ben was there already, sitting at his desk. He looked up and smiled his crooked smile as Karen went in. 'Hi!'

'Hi yourself,' she returned brightly, putting her leather satchel on the desk. 'I didn't see your car.'

'It's not here,' he said. 'Big ends went last night on the way home. I came in by bus.'

Karen was shocked at his pallor but wasn't going to let him know it. Cheerfulness was the key-word this morning. She was very fond of Ben and she hated to see him looking so wretched.

'Oh Ben, how rotten for you, I wish I'd known, I could have given you a lift home.' Home, she thought compassionately, you could hardly call Ben's house home—an empty, unwelcoming place it was now, since the divorce.

He gave her a twisted grin, pushing back his hair. Ben Clark was coming up to forty, a sturdy man with a humorous twist to his mouth and straight fair hair that flopped over his wide forehead, a forehead that was already showing deep creases—much too deep for his age, Karen thought with a sudden pang. 'It did me good to walk,' he said. 'Blew the cobwebs away. I rehearsed my speech for this morning all the way home. Don't they call it the speech on the gallows?' He pulled a ghoulish face.

'That is *not* funny, Mr Clark,' Karen said. 'I refuse to listen to such negative talk. Have you had any breakfast?'

He rubbed his left temple. 'D'you know. I really can't remember. I know the house was frigid when I got up. The boiler's gone on the blink again, I imagine.'

Poor old Ben—having to fend for himself in an icy-cold house, just when he needed someone to look after his creature comforts.

Karen opened her satchel. 'A good thing I anticipated this state of affairs.' She took out a packet of sandwiches and set it before him on the desk on a paper picnic-plate. 'Eat up.'

Ben said nothing for a moment, just stared at her with a look in his brown eyes that she was beginning to recognise. Then he shook his head in wonder. 'Karen, you're absolutely incredible.'

Lucy came in with two mugs of coffee. 'I'll make some more for when *he* comes,' she volunteered brightly.

'The name's Marston—Mr Marston,' Karen corrected. 'And don't forget to call him sir.'

Lucy gave her an old-fashioned look. 'I'm practising me curtsy,' she said and went out.

'Cheeky young so-and-so,' grinned Ben. 'We really need some discipline in this place.'

'This place,' Karen said, sitting down opposite Ben at the big desk and emptying her satchel of the papers she had taken home last night, 'is pretty good just as it is. You don't hear of any strikes at Clark's Components. Look at 'em all out there—happy as Larry, whoever *he* was.' She nodded towards the glass partition that divided the office from the big workshop, where twenty women in white overalls sat at their separate small benches, assembling the intricate bits and pieces that made up the latest electronic gadget that Ben had designed and put on the market.

His eyes followed her glance. 'Yes, they're a jolly good lot.' He was silent again, his lips pursed together, and Karen knew what he was thinking but wouldn't say: How much longer would they be sitting there working away so industriously?

He turned away abruptly and munched a sandwich. 'Um, these are jolly good. Thanks a lot, Karen.' He grinned crookedly. 'Note—the condemned man is eating a hearty breakfast.'

Karen said briskly, 'Don't be negative, Ben. Everything's going to be fine. This Saul Marston individual will be impressed, I know he will.'

'I'd like to believe it, but the books are fairly damning evidence. He'll only have to glance at the figures for the last two months to turn him off, I'm afraid.'

'That brute of a bank manager! Why did Mr Fellowes have to retire just at a bad moment for us?' Karen gulped her coffee too hot and choked.

Ben nodded ruefully. 'Yes, I know. Fellowes would probably have helped us over this particular hump. But there would have been another one pretty soon. I've faced it, I'm just not a very good manager.'

'Oh, but that's nonsense——'

Ben shook his head and a lock of fair hair flopped over his forehead. He pushed it back impatiently. 'No, it isn't nonsense, my loyal Karen. I'm not kidding myself. My real interest lies out there——' nodding towards the workshop '——not in here.' He waved a hand at the jumble of books and papers spread on the desk. 'I should have thought it out more carefully five years ago, before I decided to start up on my own. I'm just not a business man, and that's the plain truth.' His mouth twisted. 'My ex-wife was right, she was against the whole venture, but I thought I could make a go of it.'

Karen was silent, not trusting herself to speak of Christine, because she might say something she regretted. But inside she fumed as she thought of Ben's wife, with her pretty face and her petulant little mouth, who had walked out on him six months ago, about the time that things started to go wrong with the business. Just a rat leaving a sinking ship, she thought. No, worse than a rat, because a rat acted on instinct, whereas Christine Clark had calculated just what she was doing when she went off to New York with a rep from a top firm that made women's underwear.

Karen glanced at Ben's sombre face and said, 'Well—let's look on the bright side. We don't know yet what this Marston man's proposition will be. It might work out quite well.'

Ben picked up the last sandwich and said rather grimly, 'It could do—for him. He gobbles up small businesses that have got into difficulties. Adds them to his empire—that's how he made his money. We'll doubtless go the way of all the rest if he considers our products would be useful to him. I just hope he'll want to keep the girls on. As for me——' he shrugged '—I've faced it, Karen. However you look at it

Clark's Components is finished as a viable concern. I'll be redundant.'

He stretched out a hand and covered hers on the desk. 'I'm terribly sorry, my dear, I'm afraid this will affect you too. It's a devil. My only consolation is that you won't have any difficulty in finding another job. You'll have a queue forming to get your services.'

She smiled at him. She was very fond of Ben Clark; she'd been with him through all the ups and downs— mostly downs—of the last traumatic months. Very gently she disengaged her hand and began to straighten her papers.

'Thanks for the compliment, Ben, but I refuse to consider that it will be necessary. I'm going to keep my fingers crossed and hope that somehow things will go on more or less as usual. This Marston man is supposed to be an expert on the job—surely he'll recognise a good thing when he sees it. What's he like, anyway?'

Ben had met Saul Marston recently at a week-end seminar for managers, when Marston had come to talk to the group about his own ideas and experiences that had led him to the top of the business world.

Ben shrugged. 'Oh—just what you'd imagine. Success and confidence writ large all over him. A very big fish—showing all us little tiddlers how it was done.'

'How old is he? What does he look like?'

'Middle thirties, I'd think. Tallish, dark. Very much the big shot. All the usual trappings—Rolls Royce and everything that goes with it.'

Karen didn't like the picture of this Saul Marston at all. 'He sounds like an intolerable show-off.'

Ben finished the last sandwich. 'Oh, I don't know,' he said reasonably. 'You have to choose your role at the start and then you can forget it and move on to more important things. Make sure you look the part and have the props. That was one of the things he told us.'

'And what are the more important things?'

Ben looked up at the ceiling, ticking the points off on his fingers. 'Motivation—drive—knowledge of all the facts—willingness to take risks—understanding people——'

'And a healthy bank balance?'

'Or a trusting bank manager,' Ben amended drily. 'If you can inspire your bank manager with confidence then the sky's the limit.'

'H'm.' Karen drained her coffee mug and stood up. 'Well, I don't really fancy Mr Saul Marston but I'll reserve judgment until I've seen him.'

Ben looked up at her, his brown eyes soft, like a spaniel's. She wished that the similarity hadn't occurred to her, it seemed to belittle Ben somehow. 'Give him your lovely smile, Karen. That'll soften him up,' he grinned, and added, 'You're looking prettier than ever this morning. I like that red thing.'

Karen twitched her pleated skirt. 'I thought it might indicate our fighting spirit. I always feel lively when I wear red.' She twirled round. She hoped she wasn't overdoing the Little Miss Sunshine act, but really, Ben *did* need cheering up. She added a little doubtfully, 'I hope I don't look too jazzy for a personal assistant.'

'You look terrific.' Ben took his eyes from her with an obvious effort. 'I'm the one who's letting the side down.'

He walked over to the small mirror beside the curly wooden coat-stand and peered into it. 'God, I look a mess. Talk about giving the right impression to our potential benefactor! I should at least bear some resemblance to a managing director.' He drew the collar of his open-necked shirt together. 'They wear business suits. don't they, managing directors? I haven't worn a tie for ages, I hate the beastly things. Should I wear a tie, Karen?' He turned a rueful face to her. 'What's your advice?

She hesitated. 'Well . . .'

Ben grinned and raised a hand. 'Fair enough, my child, you don't need to put it into words. I shall now make my final effort. I shall go into the town and buy a shirt and a tie. I might even fit in a hair-cut. Marston's not due until eleven, is he?'

'Eleven. That's what he said in his letter. Take my car,' Karen offered.

Ben paused beside her on his way to the door. 'Thanks, Karen. Thanks for everything,' he said slowly. 'What should I do without you?' Their glances held, hers a little surprised, his almost pleading.

Then, abruptly, he grabbed his raincoat and left the office.

Karen went thoughtfully about the business of tidying up. She was twenty-three and she had seen that look in a man's eyes more times than she could remember. She didn't have to be conceited to know that she was attractive, with her dark shining hair, her fine, perfect skin, and her long-lashed hazel eyes. She had never lacked dates or hopeful partners for dances or tennis, and holidays abroad with friends had been quite exciting in a care-free way.

But Ben was different—older, more mature than most of the boys she had known. She stood still for a moment, pressing the cap of a pen against her lips. Could she be falling in love with Ben? Could this caring tenderness she felt for him develop into something deeper? She knew for a certainty that it was up to her—she had seen the question in Ben's eyes. Ben wouldn't take it further unless she encouraged him, she knew that too. She understood him so well, he was such a modest person, she could guess how he saw himself—a near-failure in business, and with a divorce just behind him. He probably thought of himself as too old for her, too. No, Ben wouldn't take the first step.

But the thought that he might want to gave her a warm feeling. Ben was such a dear, and already she loved him in an odd, comfortable sort of way. Karen had had flirtations but never experienced the wild thrill of romantic love and was inclined to discount it, having been brought up by cool, professional parents who, though affectionate, had the detached attitude towards emotion which they seemed to consider necessary to medical people.

She shook her shoulders impatiently. This was no time to consider romantic possibilities—the first thing was to be sure that the company would survive, and about this she was much more hopeful than Ben was himself. He had a good little set-up going here and he was brilliant at his job. If this Saul individual had any business sense at all (and he must have plenty!) he would recognise all this and that it only needed an infusion of capital—and perhaps some of his marvellous business expertise—to have the place flourishing and profitable.

She looked round the now immaculately tidy but rather shabby office. Well—Superman would just have to take them as he found them. The clock over the door said 9.45 and Karen went through the connecting door into the workshop.

She walked down the centre aisle between the worktables, pausing now and then to have a word with one of the workers, enquiring after a child at school, an ailing relative, the progress of a flat-purchase. They all had a smile for her and, as for herself, she never ceased to marvel at their deft fingers handling the tiny instruments and components so expertly and rapidly. They were a good lot, as Ben had said, and he took care to make their work as interesting for them as he could, explaining the end products to them if they wanted to listen, keeping them informed of new developments well in advance, through the factory manager, Charlie Benson, and his assistant, Jean McBride.

Jean came up to Karen now from the far end of the work-room, a worried-looking young woman in a navy-blue boiler-suit. She had been with the company since its start and Karen knew that both Ben and Charlie thought the world of her intelligence and her tact in acting as a sort of unofficial shop steward. Jean was a small thin girl, with light red hair and a pale, serious face. She and Karen usually hit it off well, though Karen sometimes found Jean taciturn to the point of gruffness. She had a good physics degree and was always ready to talk about her work, but her personal life remained a closed book. Except for the fact that she lived with and looked after an aged grandmother, Karen knew very little about her.

'Hullo Karen,' Jean said now. 'I'd like a word with Ben, is he in his office?'

Karen shook her head. 'He's just popped into town. He won't be long. Can I help?'

'No, not really. Give me a buzz when he gets back, will you?'

As she turned away Karen said quickly, 'He's going to be tied up for most of the morning. An important appointment.'

Jean stopped, hesitated, and then blurted out quickly, 'Karen, something's wrong, isn't it? Ben hasn't been himself lately. He's not ill, is he?'

'Ill? Why, no. At least I don't think so.' Come to think of it, she *had* noticed that Ben had been taking a lot more of his indigestion tablets lately, but that wasn't surprising, considering the strain he'd been under.

'Don't you *know*?' Jean's pale cheeks had gone faintly pink. 'I'd have thought one of the jobs of a personal assistant——' she seemed to put the words in quotes '—was to keep an eye on her chief's health.'

There was more than a hint of aggression in Jean's tone and Karen said warmly, 'I certainly should if I thought there was any way I could help him. Ben's not the kind of man to be nannied, you know.'

Jean stared at her, her eyes hostile under their light lashes. 'You don't have to tell me what kind of a man Ben is.'

She turned on the heel of her sensible brown shoes and walked rapidly away to the far end of the aisle.

Karen stood looking after her, a little frown between her brows. She and Jean had always hit it off quite well, although Jean wasn't the kind of girl you could get close to. But today she seemed really unfriendly. Karen shrugged as she went back to the office. Maybe something had gone wrong at home that was upsetting Jean—you never really knew about people's troubles unless they confided in you and you just had to make allowances.

She stood in the doorway of the office looking around it before she went in, wondering how it would appear to a tycoon like this Saul Marston. Very tatty, probably. He himself would no doubt have one of those ultra-modern offices, full of computers and word-processors and telex machines.

'We really ought to modernise in the office,' Ben had said only last month, with a disgusted look at the desk with its single telephone and the intercom he had bought three years ago and which was already out of date. But next day had come a letter from Christine's solicitor which had caused Ben to mutter under his breath about sharks, and after that no more had been said about modernising the office. Karen didn't know what was in the letter, but guessed it was a demand for money. Christine had brought the divorce suit on the grounds of unreasonable behaviour and Ben had been so shocked and unhappy about the whole wretched business that he had decided not to contest it, and the final settlement had been all in Christine's favour.

'I suppose she had a case,' Ben had said wearily to Karen, when it was all over. 'I haven't been much of a husband these last few years—working all hours of the day and night.'

'But you were doing it for her,' Karen had put in, trying to control the angry resentment she felt on Ben's behalf.

'Only partly, I'm afraid,' he had admitted. 'This place here has meant pretty well everything to me lately. No wife will stand for that.'

Karen said nothing but inside she had disagreed with him. She believed that in a good marriage there should be understanding and friendship. A time to give and a time to take. It had seemed to her that Christine had wanted to do all the taking and she would have liked to do battle on Ben's behalf and tell his spoilt little wife just what she thought of her.

But of course it hadn't been any of her business, and all she could do was to make herself as useful as possible to Ben in the months that followed the divorce. In those months he had come to rely more and more on her and she had learned all there was to learn about the administrative side of the company, which had freed Ben to devote more time to his first love—the technical side.

But it hadn't really worked, Karen thought now, sadly. She knew enough about business to understand the difficulty. It was all too small. They worked too near the margins all the time. The orders came in, but suppliers got peevish about their accounts not being paid and once or twice actually held up deliveries of materials, which meant that orders weren't met on time, customers complained, and so it went on, like a chain that got weaker and weaker in every link until it was nearly breaking. Then, inevitably, the most important link had broken. The new bank manager had finally refused to extend the overdraft. There was just enough money left to pay the girls at the end of the week and then—that would be that. Ben would have to agree to a receiver being called in. Karen felt suddenly cold as the bleak word 'bankrupt' came into her mind.

Unless—*unless*—a fairy godfather in the person of this Saul Marston came to the rescue. He *must*, Karen thought now, crossing her fingers hard as she sat down in Ben's chair. There was so much potential here, she was sure of it, the only lack was capital. Ben was brilliant at his own job—so many people said so.

Only last week he had completed work on an original gadget—an electronic component of an entirely new and advanced design. Karen opened his desk drawer and took out the big folder that contained his beautiful drawings. 'My baby,' he had said only yesterday, patting the folder lovingly, and added with his wry grin, 'I'm afraid the poor little brute is going to be stillborn.'

Karen looked at the drawings that had taken him all those weeks of concentrated work. Technically they meant nothing to her, but she knew how much they meant to Ben, and that was enough for her. She would leave them out on the desk and hope that Ben wouldn't be too modest to show them to this Saul person, when he arrived.

She began, methodically, to put the books in the order in which he would probably want to examine them, but before she had finished the office door flew open and Lucy's face appeared, her cheeks bright pink, her eyes popping out.

'He's here,' she mouthed silently, and aloud, in the primmest voice she could muster, 'Mr Marston to see Mr Clark.'

Karen's eyes went in horror to the clock over the door. It said three minutes to ten. He had said eleven, she *knew* he had. Her heart started to thud like a steam-hammer. Ben couldn't possibly be back for another half-hour, possibly more if he had gone to have a hair-cut as he'd threatened.

For a moment cold panic shook her, but only for a moment. She was Ben's personal assistant and it was the job of a personal assistant to stand in for her chief if necessary, wasn't it? Oh, but not in a life-or-death situation like this, wailed a faint voice inside her. Shut up, Karen shrieked silently at it, you can only do your best, can't you?

She drew in a quick breath. 'Ask Mr Marston to come in, Lucy.'

From a long distance she heard Lucy say. 'Will you come in, sir, please,' in an awed voice, far removed from her usual breezy tone.

Karen steadied herself. Lucy was doing her best, now it was her turn. She stood up and came round the desk, and she would have felt encouraged if she could have known the picture she presented—that of a smooth young woman executive—a tallish girl, her dark hair shining, her white blouse immaculate, her scarlet pleated skirt swishing softly round her slender legs.

She often remembered afterwards that first sight of Saul Marston and the extraordinary effect he had on her. As Lucy drew back he appeared in the doorway and immediately the office seemed smaller, shabbier. Then the background went out of focus and there was only the man standing there, tall, dark, arrogantly opulent in a pale, supple suede car-coat that just reached his thighs, topping black, fashionably-cut trousers. The whole outfit must have cost the earth. In the poorly-lit office the unsmiling eyes that met hers glinted like polished jet under thick, curving lashes. Snowflakes had settled on his thick, dark hair. There was something in the way he stood there, absolutely still, that stirred an odd sensation, almost like fear, in the pit of Karen's stomach.

The few seconds stretched into timelessness. Fear wouldn't have been altogether out of place, confronting this man. It was ridiculous, of course, but something about him seemed to spell danger.

Then Karen's secretarial training came to her rescue and she stepped forward, holding out a hand, and heard her own voice say pleasantly, 'Good morning, Mr Marston, I'm Karen Lane, Mr Clark's personal assistant. I'm afraid Mr Clark had to go into town—trouble with his car—and he isn't back yet. He shouldn't be long—perhaps you'd like a cup of coffee while you wait.'

He took her hand briefly, and again she felt that tweak of—what was it, fear?—as she experienced the hard strength of his clasp. He crossed to the desk in two strides. 'No coffee thank you and I shan't be waiting. I have only a very short time to spare. I have a meeting in London.' He picked up the drawings of Ben's new component. 'What's this?'

She stared at him blankly for a moment, taken aback by his abrupt, almost rude approach. Then she remembered that she was supposed to be backing Ben up in every possible way, and she made herself smile.

'I'm afraid I don't understand the technicalities. I just know it's a project that Mr Clark has been working on for some time. It's a—a—sort of switch, I think.'

He didn't smile back and as he raised his eyes and looked at her there was that odd, sinking feeling inside her again. 'I can see that,' he said curtly. 'Is it in production?'

Surly beast, Karen thought. How could she go on being pleasant to him? But she must, and she was on firmer ground now. 'Oh no, not yet. Mr Clark has been so busy recently——' her voice trailed off as she met his gaze—the glittering black eyes were narrowed as they fixed themselves on her face. 'But he'll be able to tell you all about it himself when he comes back.'

'Possibly.' He was looking round the office now and Karen's heart sank, seeing it as he was probably seeing it: the scratched desk, the old electric typewriter, the green metal filing cabinets that Ben had bought second-hand. And it was a disaster that only yesterday the PVC that covered the visitor's chair had split and the innards were poking through.

'Won't you sit down, Mr Marston? And perhaps you'd like to be looking through the books,' Karen suggested hastily.

He sat down opposite to her and she pushed the books and folders across the desk to him one by one. 'Order book, day book, work in progress, cash book, bank statements . . .'

He glanced briefly through each in turn, flicking the pages over almost contemptuously with one long, well-manicured finger. Karen's eyes went desperately to the side window, through which she could get a view of part of the small car-park. Ben, where are you? Please come back soon. *Please.* But all she saw were the long, graceful lines of a Rolls Royce, its radiator cap gleaming silver in the murky gloom, snow-flakes gathering on its elegant dark-green bonnet.

Suddenly she realised he had spoken. 'Balance sheet? Profit and loss account?'

She opened another folder and took out last years' audited accounts. 'This is where the crunch will come, when he sees these,' Ben had said morosely last night. 'He'll probably walk out on the spot.'

But Saul Marston didn't walk out. He lowered his head over the papers while Karen watched, fascinated, as the last remaining snow-flake melted and merged into his hair. It was thick hair, very strong and springy, the kind of hair that needs firm treatment to make it conform. Her glance travelled down to what she could see of his face from this angle. His skin was sun-tanned (winter sports, no doubt.) The wide forehead with the faintest of horizontal grooves gave his face an authoritative look, only slightly belied by those sensational lashes hiding his eyes.

Then abruptly, and to Karen's utter confusion, he raised his eyes and looked across the desk at her, not lifting his head. She flinched as if she had received a sword-thrust, but his voice, when he spoke, was quiet. 'These figures are pretty damning,' he said. 'Have you any observations to make about them?'

Oh Ben, how should I answer that?

She swallowed. 'Do you mean can I justify them? Explain them?'

She thought she saw a flicker of amusement in the jet-black eyes. Oh no, Mr Saul Marston, you're not going to patronise me. 'I'd have thought they were self-explanatory, to a man of your experience,' she said quite calmly. 'Our difficulty is with cashflow. As you can see, we're trying to work on a capital that is much too small for the potentially expanding side of the business.'

He was watching her as she spoke, his face expressionless. She couldn't judge whether he was annoyed or not by her flash of brief defensive spirit. He sat back in his chair. 'You sum it up admirably,' he said. 'Won't the bank manager play ball?'

Karen spread out her hands. 'Not any longer.'

'H'm—well—he probably knows what he's doing.' He was standing up now. He's going, Karen thought desperately. He's just going to walk out and all Ben's hopes and chances are going with him. She jumped to her feet and flew round the desk to stand between Saul Marston and the door.

'Mr Marston, please don't go yet. Please don't make up your mind until you've seen Ben—Mr Clark.' The words tumbled out; her cheeks were pink; her hazel eyes very bright. 'This is really an excellent set-up here. We have lots of good customers and plenty more showing interest. The staff are marvellous—loyal and dependable and highly skilled. And Mr Clark himself is really a brilliant designer—everyone says so.' She paused, breathing rather fast, her eyes searching his impassive face. 'Won't you come round the workshop and see for yourself?'

Again she saw amusement in the black depths of his eyes. 'You make a good advocate, Miss Lane,' he said. He shrugged slightly. 'O.K., lead on.'

Karen's knees were like jelly as she opened the door into the workshop and she breathed a silent prayer of relief when she saw Charlie Benson, the works manager, standing at one of the assembly tables nearby.

She called to him and he came across to where they stood. 'Mr Marston this is our works' manager, Mr Benson. Charlie, Mr Marston would like to see everything that's going on here. Would you take him round and answer any questions he has?'

'O.K., Miss Lane.' Charlie gave her his cheery grin and glanced at the man who stood beside her. Charlie was nobody's fool and he had a knack for summing people up; he was seldom wrong. 'This way, sir.' His voice held a certain deference. Karen stood and watched them walk away together, Charlie small and amiable, chatting happily as they moved from one table to the next. Saul Marston nodding briefly, pausing now and again for a word with one of the girls.

Well, at least he was *looking*, that was something. There certainly wouldn't be anything he could fault in the workshop, however dismal the books and accounts might be. She went back into the office and peered out of the window. The snow was gathering thickly now on the bonnet of the Rolls, but her own little Mini, with Ben inside, was nowhere to be seen.

'That's it then, Miss Lane.' Saul Marston's deep, clipped voice came from behind her and she spun round.

'Won't you wait a little longer?' Karen made a last effort. 'Mr Clark should be here any moment now.'

'No point,' he said briefly. 'I've seen all I want to see.' He picked up Ben's drawings and studied them again for a couple of minutes in silence. Then he put them down carefully on the desk and walked towards the door. 'Thank you for your help, Miss Lane. You've told me all I want to know.'

Karen felt like death. This was how it must feel to stand in the dock and hear the judge pronouncing sentence. No hope. Nothing she could do now.

But what could she say to Ben when he came back? She put her hand into the big, strong hand that Saul Marston was extending and somehow managed to frame the words that would surely get some response from him. Something she could tell Ben. 'What——' she began. 'What do you think?'

Saul Marston stood there in his fabulous suede jacket, his immaculately-cut trousers and hand-made leather shoes, breathing affluence from every inch of him and looked slowly round the shabby office, at the desk littered with account books that told their own damning story.

He shrugged. 'It's—pathetic,' he said.

Her eyes widened and she could have struck out at him, only he was still holding her hand. She wanted to scream at him, 'Get out, get *out*, you arrogant bastard, and don't come back.' But of course she didn't; she just stood there, hating him. She had never felt such violent loathing of anybody before in her whole life.

He looked at her with that narrowed, assessing look. 'How's your shorthand?' He shot the question at her.

'Excellent.' Her tone was equally clipped.

'Yes,' he said. 'I thought it would be.' He paused thoughtfully and she realised that her hand was still enclosed in his. She wanted to drag it away but was quite helpless to do so. He went on looking at her for what seemed an age before he said, 'What on earth is a bright girl like you doing working in a dump like this? If you ever consider coming to London, get in touch with me. I could always find you a spot in one of my companies.'

She found her voice then and she could almost hear the ice rattling in it. 'Thank you, Mr Marston,' she said. 'I shan't be taking you up on that.'

'No?' The dark brows lifted. 'Pity.' Then, slowly, and for the first time, he smiled at her and she almost fainted as the impact of that smile slithered through her body. It started in his eyes, creasing them at the corners as the long dark lashes lowered, then pulled at his long, sensuous lips, showing teeth white against the brown of his skin. A devastating, utterly shattering smile.

'Tell Mr Clark I'll be in touch,' he said. He released her hand and went out of the office. A moment later she heard the purr of the Rolls outside and then he was gone.

Karen stood quite still, rubbing weakly at the hand that had been enclosed in his, feeling as if a great green tidal wave had washed over her. When Lucy's pink face appeared round the door she blinked at her stupidly.

'Cor!' Lucy grinned. 'What about that, then? Quite something, wasn't he?'

'What?' Karen mumbled. 'What did you say?'

Lucy's blue eyes widened knowingly. 'I'll make you some more coffee,' she said. 'You look as if you need it.'

The coffee helped and Karen's wits had returned by the time Ben came back into the office ten minutes later. He glanced at the clock. 'Made it with time to spare,' he announced. 'How do I look, ducky?'

He minched across the office in imitation of a model on the catwalk. He wore a new white shirt with a jaunty blue-striped tie and his fair hair had been trimmed and brushed flat to his head. 'Everyone's idea of a managing director, what?'

Oh God, Karen thought, how can I tell him? He was trying so hard. Putting on such a brave act.

'Ben——' she began. 'Oh, Ben . . .'

She felt the tears stinging behind her eyes and bit her lip hard. But it was too late. Karen, who hadn't cried for years, put her head down on the desk and burst into tears.

CHAPTER TWO

'You mean he didn't say anything? Nothing at all? Didn't give you any hint of what was in his mind?'

An hour had passed and Ben sat slumped in his chair, drinking his second mug of coffee and trying, Karen saw only too well, not to give way to despair.

'Not really.' Karen wouldn't meet his eyes. 'He was a man of few words.' She managed a small grin.

'Yes. I can believe that. But he must have said something—something to upset you.' His brown eyes softened. 'I never saw you cry before, Karen.'

She shook her head. 'That was just me being silly. I'd been horribly tense and worked up all the time he was here. I'd been so anxious not to do or say anything to put him off. I suppose when he'd gone the reaction just got to me, that's all.'

'I blame myself,' he said morosely. 'I should never have left the office. I should have known that he might come early.'

'How could you know?' Karen argued. 'His letter said eleven—you remember, we checked it again—and people aren't usually an hour early for an appointment.' She wondered if that had been a nasty, clever ploy on Saul Marston's part. If he had turned up early to surprise them—to see exactly what was going on when they weren't expecting him. It was just the kind of dirty trick he would play, she thought, her lip curling with distaste.

'Tell me again all that happened—all that he said.'

She'd been through it half-a-dozen times already but now she went patiently through it again. It was an edited version she gave Ben. Nothing could have made her repeat the horrid words that man had used. *Pathetic*, he'd said. *A dump*, he'd said, with that superior expression on his handsome face. She boiled inside again as she remembered.

'He went round the workshop quite carefully,' she ended her report, 'and he talked to Jean and to some of the girls. And he seemed to get on with Charlie. He looked twice at those new drawings of yours too. He seemed interested in them.'

'But he looked at the accounts too, of course,' Ben reminded her wryly.

'Well, that was partly what he came for, after all.' Karen used her most reasonable tone. 'I mean, you wouldn't have approached him in the first place if the financial side of the business had been going swimmingly, would you?'

'No, I suppose not,' Ben sighed. Then he seemed to make an effort to cheer up. 'Look, I couldn't settle down to work this morning. Marston can't possibly get in touch just yet if he's driving back to London to a meeting. Suppose I treat you to lunch?' He grinned and fingered his new tie. 'I can't waste all this finery, and you look smashing, Karen. We'll knock 'em for six in the Grand snack-bar. Let's go and drink to the good news, what do you say?'

She wanted to weep again but instead she smiled. 'Thanks, Ben, that would be lovely,' she said. 'I'll go and get my coat on.'

It was just after three o'clock that afternoon when the phone on Ben's desk rang and Karen went across the office to answer it. Each time the phone had rung since they got back from lunch she had gone cold and now her fingers were damp on the stem of the receiver as she picked it up.

'Good afternoon, Clark's Components.' She held her stomach tight, as if she were expecting a blow.

A woman's voice said, 'I have a call for Mr Ben Clark. Mr Marston would like to speak to him.'

'I'll tell him. Will you hold the line for a moment please.' This was it, then. This was the crunch that had to come. As she pushed open the door into the workshop Karen's knees were shaking.

Ben was standing just the other side of the glass partition. 'Telephone for you.' Karen said, and when his eyes opened wide and his fair brows rose questioningly she nodded, tight-lipped.

He got the message and she thought he squared his shoulders slightly before he walked steadily back into the office.

Karen stayed in the workshop. Ben must have time to adjust to what he was going to hear, she couldn't intrude. And she couldn't bear to see his face as he listened to what Saul Marston was going to say to him. If and when Ben needed her he would call for her.

Jean and Charlie Benson were working together at the far end of the workshop and Karen avoided that corner. She didn't want any more questions from Jean just at this moment.

She wandered up and down the aisles. It was strange that you could get so attached to a place as prosaic as a factory workshop, but over the years it had grown so familiar that it was part of her life and she loved it. The faintly antiseptic smell of the floor-cleaner that the daily woman used; the work-desks, each with its own shaded light below which the nimble fingers of the girls moved so expertly; she knew every inch of the floor space, every note of the taped music that moaned softly from a loudspeaker in one corner. They'd had those tapes for ages, she thought now, she

must really see about ordering some new ones. Then
she remembered, and a darkness closed down.

Not that it showed anywhere but in her own mind—
the girls all seemed to be in a particularly happy mood
today, and a buzz of chat and a ripple of laughter
sounded now and again between the desks. Mrs
Grayson, a part-timer who was one of their best
workers, looked up as Karen approached. 'Don't
worry, Miss Lane,' she smiled. 'We're getting on with
the work. It's Doreen's birthday today, that's what all
the excitement's about, and she's going to get her
engagement ring this evening.'

'Oh, how splendid, I must go and congratulate her.'

For as long as it took to talk to young Doreen and
take pleasure in her radiant happiness, Karen forgot
everything else. Then Doreen said shyly, 'I think Mr
Clark wants you, Miss Lane,' and Karen spun round
to see Ben standing in the office entrance door, waving
to her.

She went straight to the chair at her desk and sank
into it. Ben closed the office door behind her and as he
turned back she could hardly believe what she saw.
His blue eyes were shining and he was beaming all
over his face.

He made a thumbs-up sign. 'We may be home and
dry,' he said.

Karen could only stare at him blankly. Her inside
felt as if she had taken a step up in the dark that wasn't
there at all.

'Marston was most encouraging,' Ben paced up and
down the office, brimming with nervous energy. 'Oh,
not with the office set-up or the business accounts—
those were all rubbish as far as he was concerned. He
actually said that it was a pity that we were
functioning on such a pathetically small budget when
we had such an excellent product—or maybe several

products, for he seemed quite taken with my new idea here.' He patted the drawings that were still laid out on the desk.

'He asked me a lot of questions,' Ben went on, perching on the edge of the desk beside Karen. 'Whether we had room to expand here—take on more staff, and of course I said yes. Then he wanted to know about the cash situation—whether I'd be prepared for one of his accountants to come in and take over the immediate day-to-day cash affairs, underpinned by his own credit-worthiness. That would be temporary—for the time I was away.'

'Away?' Karen echoed faintly. 'Tell me slowly, Ben, I can take it all in at once.'

'He wants me to sit in on a conference next week,' Ben said triumphantly. 'Fly out to Mexico, all expenses paid. Acapulco, believe it or not, where all the lovely people go to play. That's the kind of spot that blokes like Saul Marston choose for their conferences. He wants me to meet the directors of the other companies in his group. He thinks my stuff may be of interest to some of them.'

He went round and sank into his chair and suddenly his eyes were glassy, his shoulders slumped. 'It's too much all at once, Karen love. I can't believe it's really happening.'

I can't either, Karen thought. She felt like a pricked balloon. She'd been all buoyed up, expecting to hear the worst, to try to console Ben, or at least to stick by him. And now—this. She had certainly misjudged the enigmatic Saul Marston, but her dislike of him hadn't changed one little bit. Had he deliberately misled her? she wondered. Or was he just the kind of man who liked to adopt a Sphinx-like outward approach? Did he think it added to his wonderful mystique? Oh, she thought angrily, he was just hateful.

'It's wonderful,' she said. 'Marvellous news. When do you go?'

'Thursday. The tickets will be booked and waiting to be picked up at Heathrow. And he'll be in Mexico City himself when we arrive. The plan is to contact him there and we'll all go on to Acapulco together.'

'Sounds like an exciting trip.' Karen said. 'I'm so very glad for you, Ben. You deserve success.' She *was* glad, of course she was. It was just that she would have been happier if the saviour of the company had been someone less intolerable than the intolerable Saul Marston. Still, it wasn't likely that she would have to encounter him much—perhaps never again. He wouldn't be visiting this minor addition to his empire very often. 'I'll hold the fort here while you're away, of course, and be of any assistance I can to this accountant person, whoever he is.'

Ben lifted his head. 'But—didn't I tell you—you're coming with me, Karen.'

She was stunned into silence for several moments. Then, 'Me?' she croaked. 'Oh no, Ben, you must have got it wrong. Why should I come?'

He shook his head, smiling. 'Because I can't do without you,' he said softly. Then he laughed. 'No, Karen, that's just my personal feeling. What Marston said was, "Bring that assistant of yours along. We need a bright girl like that to take minutes of the meetings and supervise reports. We'll get temporary typists out there but we must have someone capable of taking charge and collating the whole proceedings." He thought you could make a good job of that, Karen. And so do I.' Ben chuckled delightedly. 'Your passport's O.K.? Good. Then off we go on Thursday.' He closed his eyes. 'It'll be like a marvellous holiday, in between the meetings. We'll savour the luxurious delights of Acapulco. Lie on the beach, swim in the blue, blue Pacific. It'll be high season there in January.'

He got up and came and stood behind her chair and put both hands on her shoulders, giving her a little hug. 'What do you say, Karen?'

She swallowed, staring straight ahead. She should be enthusing with him, agreeing eagerly. But something was standing in the way, a vague, threatening presentiment of danger ahead. And it seemed to be personified in the tall, dark, inscrutable form of Saul Marston.

He must have been planning this in his mind even before he left here this morning. That was why he had said, 'How's your shorthand?' He must have known what he intended to do—and yet he hadn't given her a clue when she asked him. He had even misled her, quite deliberately it seemed to her now.

'I—I can't quite take it in all at once,' she stammered. 'I never expected—look, Ben, it isn't that I don't want to come, but do you mind if I talk it over with my parents this evening before I finally decide? I could let you know in the morning.'

There was a short pause and she knew he was disappointed. But he said, 'No, of course I don't mind, if that's what you want.' His hands dropped from her shoulders and he moved away.

He turned over the papers on the desk absently, not looking at them. Then he said abruptly, 'Would you be very sweet and not wait until the morning to let me know? Give me a ring at home tonight when you've decided. It doesn't matter how late it is. Will you do that?'

She nodded. She was playing for time, she knew. Neither of her parents would put obstacles in the way. And if, when she had thought it over, the answer was

No, then it might be easier not to have to face Ben when she told him. 'I'll do that,' she promised.

Asking her parents for their opinion was a formality, as Karen had thought it would be. Her father, a large good-humoured man, tired after a long evening surgery, had smiled rather absently and said, 'Very nice for you, my dear, it'll do you good to have a break. Will you need any jabs?' And when Karen said no, there was only smallpox advised and she had had a booster last year, he had nodded his head and slumped into his armchair, his nose in the British Medical Journal.

Her mother breezed in from the hospital later. Dr Esther Lane, a slim, tawny-haired woman, specialised in child psychiatry and Karen often felt slightly overawed by her successful, enthusiastic mother, who never seemed to be tired, however long and difficult her work day.

'Good for you, Karen,' she cried when her daughter broke the news. 'It'll be a splendid experience for you. Come along into the kitchen and we'll make some supper and you can tell me all about it. How about that then, James? We have a clever daughter, it seems.'

Dr James Lane laid down his medical journal and said mildly, 'But I always knew that, my dear.'

His wife shrugged off her sheepskin coat and threw it carelessly over the back of a chair. 'I take back all I ever said about dead-end jobs, Karen,' she said gaily. She had been disappointed when Karen had elected to do secretarial training instead of going on to university, but both her parents believed in allowing her to make her own choices.

As they prepared supper together in the kitchen Karen's mother bombarded her with questions. Who was this Saul Marston and what would be the position with regard to Clark's now? How would Karen's own job be affected? Was there any chance of her moving to work for Mr Marston?

'Oh, I hope not,' Karen said, cutting into a loaf somewhat viciously. 'As a matter of fact I didn't care for the man at all. He was far too pleased with himself. Too much the successful entrepreneur that we hear about all the time.'

Dr Lane pulled a knowing face. 'We need all the successful entrepreneurs we can get in this country,' she said firmly. 'What's the good of doing anything if you're not successful? I'm very glad this break has come for you, Karen. And for Mr Clark as well,' she added as an afterthought. 'As you know I never thought he would make very much of that company of his. He never seemed to me to have the necessary drive.'

Karen wasn't going to argue with her mother about Ben—it was an old point of disagreement between them. 'Mr Marston has plenty of drive anyway,' she laughed. 'But I'm not sure that I like him.'

Her mother tipped a basinful of beaten eggs into sizzling fat in an omlette pan, deftly wielding a spatula. 'Well, you don't have to like him,' she pointed out practically, 'but you'd be an idiot to miss an opportunity like this. Now, how about clothes? You'll need something really dashing for Acapulco. It'll be high season there. Your last summer dresses won't do at all.' She folded chopped mushrooms into the omlette in the pan. 'Four light dresses should do for the daytime—a couple of cocktail dresses—you can take that little white jacket for evenings. And you'll want beachwear and——'

'Mother—stop,' Karen laughed helplessly. 'This is a business trip. I'm going out as Ben's P.A.—not as a film star!'

'Nevertheless you need to look good.' Dr Lane carried plates to the table. 'We'll go into town and do a shop on Saturday, Karen, Now, run into the living-room and tell Daddy that supper's ready.'

Going to summon her father, Karen thought ruefully that her mind had been made up for her. But she had to admit that her mother had only confirmed what she herself had already decided. Even her dislike of Saul Marston couldn't weigh in the balance against the interesting and glamorous prospect of a week in Acapulco. And even more important, Ben really wanted to have her with him and she couldn't let Ben down.

She would ring him after supper and tell him she would go.

On Wednesday afternoon Ben called a meeting of all the staff in his office, even down to the boys in the despatch department. They gathered round the desk and against the walls and Karen thought the more senior of them looked faintly apprehensive. The dreaded word 'redundancy' seemed to be floating in the air.

But Ben's first words dispelled the atmosphere of uneasiness. He perched on the desk in his easy, friendly way, and looked around the crowded office with a smile. 'I've asked you all to come in because there may be a few changes in the pipe-line that I think you should know about. The fact is that the time seems to be coming when we shall have to think about expand-ing, and there are plans to form some sort of tie-up with a consortium of companies headed by Mr Saul Marston. Some of you may have met Mr Marston when he came here a day or two ago. Now let me say, first of all, that none of you need worry about your jobs—the change won't affect them in any way at all.'

An audible sigh of relief sounded round the office. 'Nothing has been finalised yet,' Ben went on. 'I'm going away tomorrow for a few days to attend a conference in Mexico and I'm taking Karen along with me.' He threw a brief smile in her direction. 'I shall know more about the plans when I come back and I promise to keep you all in the picture. While I'm away one of Mr Marston's accountants, Mr Ward, will be in charge of the office. I think that's about all for the moment. Thank you for coming. If anyone has any questions I'll do my best to answer them, but there isn't much more I can tell you just now.'

There was a buzz of talk as the staff filed out of the office on their way back to the workshop. 'Charlie,' Ben called the workshop manager back. 'Hang on a bit, will you. And Jean . . .'

Ben indicate a couple of chairs. Charlie pulled out a chair for Jean and she sat down abruptly, turning her back on Karen, who had been at her own desk across the office while Ben had been speaking.

Ben leaned forward across the desk towards them. 'I just wanted to say that—for all practical purposes— I'm leaving you two in charge. This Mr Ward will be here to keep track of the office, but he won't take any responsibility for the workshop. Any decisions that have to be made about the work in hand will be your province, Charlie.' He turned to Jean with a smile. 'And I'm sure you'll cope with any staff matters that crop up, Jean, with your usual tact and understanding.'

Karen saw Jean's pale cheeks flush and her eyes were fixed on Ben with an intent, almost yearning gaze.

'O.K.?' Ben stood up as Charlie and Jean murmured their assent. He was thanking them now for their loyalty and support, shaking them both by the hand, promising good times ahead for everyone. When they had left the office, closing the door behind them, Ben sank back into his chair and pushed his hair back with a shaking hand.

Karen saw that there were beads of sweat on his brow and he was very pale. She jumped up and went across to him. 'Are you all right, Ben?'

He pulled out a handkerchief and mopped his face. 'I'm fine,' he said, but he didn't look fine, she thought, he looked quite ill. He grinned weakly at her. 'All this excitement's too much for me.' He sat in silence for a moment, then he looked up at Karen and said, 'I hope I didn't overdo the pep-talk. After all, nothing's definitely concluded yet. God, it would be awful if I had to let them down in the end.'

'You won't have to let them down,' Karen told him firmly, resting a hand on his shoulder. 'I've got a feeling in my bones.'

He reached up and covered her hand briefly with his. 'Bless you, my child.'

She moved away to her desk and started to put her papers together.

'Karen.' Ben's voice came from behind her and he sounded odd—different.

'Yes?' She swivelled her chair round as he came over to her.

For a moment he stood staring down at her, saying nothing. Then the words seemed to be forced out of him. 'Karen, I didn't mean to say this yet but I find I have to.'

She looked up at him, surprised by the tenseness in his voice. There was a moment's silence and then he went on, 'Karen dear, I think you must know how I feel about you. You're just the most wonderful thing that ever happened in my life—a girl who's really kind—and warm—and genuine. 'You're——' he made a funny little gesture '—oh, everything.'

'Ben——' she began. It was stupid to feel embarrassed but he had never spoken to her so personally before. Their relationship had been close, but with the special closeness of a boss and his valued secretary. This was something different.

He held up a hand. 'No, hear me out now I've begun. You know how bleak things have been lately for me. I had nothing to offer any woman. But now— if things go right—if the company survives and prospers—if I can be free to go ahead with my own work—well, who knows? Perhaps our trip to Acapulco could be the beginning of something really good for us both.'

Abruptly he gripped both her hands. 'Could it, do you think? Or am I jumping the gun?'

He was watching her face closely and he looked like a man who sees daylight at the end of a long, dark tunnel and can hardly dare to believe it. She wanted to throw her arms round him and hug him and tell him that everything was going to come right at last, but he shook his head quickly and released her hands. 'That was an unfair question and you don't have to answer it. In fact, I'd rather you didn't.' He pulled a wry face of self-mockery, 'Let me keep on hoping—it gives me something to hang on to. Now, run along and finish your packing and I'll pick you up tomorrow morning as arranged. Good night, Karen.'

She hesitated, but already he was standing by his desk, turning over papers, not looking at her.

'Good night, Ben,' Karen said, and everything was the same as usual between them.

The same—and quite different.

*   *   *

Karen had never travelled further afield than Europe before, and the long flight to Mexico City next day seemed never-ending. It was a boon and a blessing that their tickets had turned out to be Business Class—that middle-way between Tourist and the exclusive First Class—which meant more comfortable seats with plenty of room between them, even a few empty seats in their compartment. At the start of the flight Ben had been talkative, eager to discuss the possibilities of the meetings that lay ahead, making tentative plans for reorganising the factory, taking on another building, perhaps. But as the hours went by he had got quieter and quieter. Karen had leafed through magazines, watched part of the film that was showing, slept on and off, and eaten the meals that were served, but Ben had only picked at his food and had nothing to drink at all.

A stewardess came along, trundling her trolley with drinks and snacks. Karen glanced at Ben but he didn't open his eyes. He looked very pale indeed, and Karen suddenly remembered Jean saying that he hadn't been himself lately, and wondering if he was ill.

The stewardess paused beside their seats, looked at Ben with a little frown, and then leaned towards Karen. 'Is he not feeling well?' she whispered. 'He doesn't look too good.'

'I don't know——' Karen began, and then Ben made a convulsive sort of movement and pitched forward in his seat, his hands round his stomach.

Karen felt suddenly cold. 'Ben—what is it—are you ill?'

He opened his eyes and groaned. 'God—I've got the most awful—pain——' His face was paper-white and beads of sweat ran down his forehead on to his cheeks.

The stewardess was wonderful. She went away and was back in a couple of seconds with a young officer in uniform who took control of everything. Karen could do nothing but hold Ben's hand and wait with growing anxiety. Ben was shivering now and rugs were brought and tucked in round him. The stewardess brought a bowl of water and sponged his face, while the officer looked on, eyes narrowed, obviously assessing the situation. Ben's face was contorted with pain and he was rocking his body and still clutching his stomach.

Karen turned a stricken face to the young officer. 'What is it, do you think? It—it isn't a heart attack, is it?'

The officer rubbed his cheek, his eyes fixed on Ben. 'I'm pretty sure it isn't. I've seen several coronaries and the signs aren't the same at all. Possibly appendix, but that's only a guess.'

'What can we *do*?' Karen urged.

He glanced at his watch. 'We're due in in just over half an hour. I think I'd better consult the captain about this. Won't be long,' he said, and disappeared down the aisle.

He returned promptly. A hospital had been contacted in Mexico City, he told Karen. An ambulance would meet the plane and Ben would have priority treatment.

The half-hour that followed was a nightmare. The stewardess was kind and sympathetic, and her calmness helped Karen to keep calm herself, but the worst part was having to see Ben suffering and being helpless to do anything but sit beside him and hold his hand and try to think of words of encouragement.

'It must be something you've eaten,' she said, and tried to remember an article she had read recently about allergies.

But Ben wasn't listening. 'Karen,' he whispered as the pain eased for a moment. 'Promise me— something.'

'Yes of course.' She pressed his hand hard.

'Carry on without me—go and see Marston—keep the flag flying—promise——' his face screwed up again.

'I promise, Ben. I'll do everything I can until you're well again. Now, *don't worry* and you'll get over this all the sooner.' He opened his eyes and fixed them on her face. 'Bless you, Karen—wonderful girl . . .' he muttered so low she could hardly hear the words.

At last the big plane came in to land and after that Karen could only stand by while the ambulance crew came aboard and attended to Ben. The other passengers in the compartment had kept considerately in the background, except for one or two concerned enquiries, and now they held back until Ben had been taken off the plane. The young officer went with Karen to rush her through the formalities in record time.

'You'll have to come back later to pick up your luggage,' he told her, 'then you can go along in the ambulance now.'

'Thank you, you've been wonderful,' Karen told him warmly and he flushed bright pink. 'Pleasure,' he mumbled. 'Hope he'll be O.K.' He turned and walked away quickly. He was a very young officer.

The only good thing about the anxious time that followed was that Karen had elected to study Spanish instead of the more usual French at secretarial school. It meant now that she could at least make herself understood, more or less, to the ambulance men, and later at the hospital, after Ben had been carried away to the Emergency Ward.

A pretty, dark-eyed nurse brought her a cup of coffee as she sat and waited nervously for news of Ben. 'How is he?' Karen tried her Spanish, but the nurse quite obviously didn't know. She shook her head and said that *el medico* would be coming to speak to Karen.

An hour dragged by before the doctor arrived, during which time Karen felt more and more weak and dizzy with nerves as the constant stream of nurses and doctors and patients and trolleys passed along the corridor of the huge hospital. But at last a white-coated man's figure paused in front of her.

'You are *la señora* Clark?' The doctor was a small thin man, who didn't look particularly interested. But thank heaven he spoke English.

Karen got to her feet. 'No, I am Karen Lane, Mr Clark's secretary. I am travelling with him to a conference. How is he, please?'

The doctor took her to a small office further along the corridor and proceeded to fire questions at her. What was Mr Clark's home address? Nearest relative? Had he been having medical advice recently? Did she know if he was receiving treatment for a stomach ulcer? Had he eaten anything on the flight and if so what?

Bemused, Karen answered as best she could but when the doctor got to his feet as a sort of signal that the interview was over she could contain herself no longer. 'Please,' she begged. 'Please tell me how he is. Can I see him? What is going to happen?'

The doctor's dark eyes regarded her narrowly. 'You are Mr Clark's secretary, did you say? Ah!' He looked horribly knowing as she nodded.

All right, all right, think what you like, Karen almost shouted at him, but that wouldn't have done any good. '*Please*.' She grabbed the sleeve of his white coat and shook it. 'Can I see him?'

He paused maddeningly, smiling at her urgency as if she were a small child. 'For two minutes only,' he said. He went back into the corridor and summoned a nurse. '*la señorita* may see Mr Clark for two minutes,' he said.

Ben was in a small side ward and a nurse was standing by his bed. He looked terrible, Karen thought with a pang, but at least he wasn't now writhing in pain. Perhaps he had been sedated. When she leaned over him and said, 'Ben—Ben dear, it's Karen,' he opened his eyes and tried to smile at her.

'This is—is—rotten for you.' She had to lean closer to hear the slurred words. 'I'll be—O.K.'

'Yes, of course you will, Ben. Very soon. This seems a wonderful hospital, I'm sure they'll give you the very best treatment.'

'Karen . . .'

'Yes, Ben?'

There was a pause as if he were gathering his strength. 'I—love—you.' The words came slowly, painfully. She leaned down and kissed his cheek and there were tears in her eyes. 'I love you too,' she whispered, 'Get better soon.' The nurse touched her shoulder and she stood up and went out of the room.

In the corridor she stood quite still, trying to gather her wits together and form some plan of action. What she wanted to do was to stay here until she knew what was going to happen, so that she could be near him. But that wasn't going to help Ben. The only way she could help him was to do as he so obviously wanted her to do—make contact with Saul Marston as they had been instructed to do. Slowly she walked away down the long corridor and eventually, by following signs, made her way to the reception hall. Again her knowledge of the language helped and a friendly porter took her to a telephone and even dialled the number of Saul Marston's hotel for her.

A female voice replied. Yes, Mr Marston was in, she would ask him to come to the 'phone. Karen stood gripping the receiver as if it were a poisonous snake, her heart thumping wildly. If only it hadn't been *him*! If it had been someone kindly and understanding!

'Yes?' Just the single word but she would have recognised his voice anywhere, deep and aloof.

She gulped in air. 'Mr Marston? This is Karen Lane.' She tried to steady her voice. She mustn't let him know she was near to panic—the first job of a personal assistant was to be cool in a crisis. 'I'm afraid we have a problem.' That was the jargon, wasn't it?

'Yes?' he said again. She could see him standing there, his dark face impassive—suspicious almost.

'Our flight got in an hour or so ago and unfortunately Mr Clark is in hospital. He was suddenly taken rather ill on the plane. I've been with him but I can't find out yet from the doctors what the trouble is. So you see, he won't be able to contact you this evening, as arranged.'

There was a very short silence. Then he said, 'Where are you speaking from? The hospital? Which one?'

Thank goodness she had asked the name of the hospital. When she told him he said crisply, 'Right. You hang on there. I'll be with you very soon. 'Bye, Karen.'

She looked at the receiver in a dazed way before she replaced it. He was coming—he was actually bothering to come. And he had called her Karen. Something in the way he had said her name gave her an odd feeling. Slowly she walked out into the big reception hall and sat down near the entrance doors to wait.

She didn't have to wait long. She saw him before he saw her, striding across the hall towards the row of seats, tall and dynamic, in black jeans and a lightweight jacket, looking very much in control of himself and everything around him. She got to her feet as he approached and as he saw her his rather grim expression changed and he smiled. His smile had the same effect on her as it had had before—back in the office at home. It made her knees go rubbery and she almost sat down again. But he was standing in front of her now, holding out both his hands.

She found her own two hands grasped and held and he said, 'Poor Karen, this is one hell of a welcome to Mexico for you both. Now, let's sit down and you can tell me the score.'

She was thankful to sink back into her chair. This was the very last thing she had expected—that he should show sympathy. He took the chair beside her and in a couple of minutes had extracted from her all she could tell him of the situation.

He questioned her gravely, nodding now and again, and when she had told him all she could, he said, 'Right, now let's get some sense out of these doctors, shall we? Come on.'

In the following half-hour Karen saw why Saul Marston had arrived at the pinnacle of success so comparatively early in life. He was a man who got what he wanted, apparently without effort. She watched while he charmed his way up through the hierarchy of a huge hospital and finally ended up talking to the surgeon in charge of Ben's case. They were talking in Spanish—Saul Marston no doubt spoke several languages perfectly—and too quickly for Karen to follow what the surgeon was saying. After a moment or two she gave up and watched Saul's face for clues as to Ben's condition. It told her nothing.

'*Muchas gracias, señor. Adios.*' Saul said finally and the surgeon bowed to them both and walked away.

Karen grabbed Saul's arm, hardly conscious that she was doing so. 'Oh, what did he say? Do they know what's the matter with Ben?'

He looked down at her thoughtfully. 'Can I get this clear from the start? Exactly what is between you and Ben Clark?'

Her eyes widened. 'I can't see that it concerns you,' she said and he sighed impatiently as they started to walk together down the long corridor.

'Of course it concerns me, you silly girl, and for goodness sake don't start going all feminine and prickly on me. If you and Ben are living together then it puts a slightly different complexion on how we all relate to each other from now on.'

'Well, we're not,' she said shortly. 'Ben and I are business associates and good friends as well, that's all. But I'm very fond of him,' she added, not able to keep the note of defiance out of her voice.

'I'll bear that in mind,' he said dryly, walking on a little ahead of her.

They climbed down a long flight of stairs and when they reached the reception area Karen stopped dead. 'I'm not going another step until you tell me what you found out from that surgeon,' she said.

'First things first,' he said. 'Where's your luggage?'

'Oh lord,' Karen gasped. 'I'd forgotten about that. It's all at the airport, every last bit of it, including our hand baggage. One of the officers on the plane promised to look after it for me so that I could go straight into the ambulance with Ben.'

'Right,' said Saul. 'We'll get a taxi and go there first. I'll give you the surgeon's report on the way.'

A few minutes later, a salmon-coloured taxi was bearing them through the traffic-laden streets. Karen was hardly conscious of the scene outside the window as she turned to Saul. 'Now,' she said. 'Please tell me about Ben. Is it something bad?'

'Bad enough,' he said. 'It seems that he's suffering from a gastric ulcer—probably been neglecting it for some time—and now it's perforated and there's considerable haemorrhage. Which means an immediate operation. They're going to get on with it straight away.'

'Oh!' Karen sank limply back in her corner, feeling icy cold.

Saul Marston's dark eyes fastened on her but he didn't say another word until they reached the airport. He leaned forward to speak to the driver, then he said, 'The taxi will wait, and I'm going to leave you to wait in it while I sort out the luggage. Just give me any papers you have and leave the rest to me.'

'But——' Karen began. She couldn't just chicken out; this was her responsibility.

Very briefly her hand was covered by a large, firm, masculine one. 'Do as you're told,' Saul Marston said. 'You can argue with me later on. This is one occasion when a male chauvinist comes in quite useful.'

'I didn't think . . .' Karen gasped. But she had, of course. That was exactly what she'd been thinking of him from the first moment she saw him. A perfect pattern of a male chauvinist, she'd thought, and everything he had done and said since then had confirmed that opinion.

'Stay here and don't move,' he told her, getting out of the taxi. 'I'll be back as soon as I can.'

Utterly exhausted, and quite incapable of putting up a fight against this overwhelming individual, Karen lay back against the leather seat of the taxi and closed her eyes. I'll just let him take charge of me this once, she thought hazily. But when I'm back to normal— then I'll show him.

What she would show him she didn't quite know. She mustn't antagonise him because that would be letting Ben down. Poor Ben, she thought with a pang of pity. Just about everything seemed to be going wrong for him. Somehow—she didn't know how—she was going to do her best to put it right, and if that meant deferring to the great Saul Marston—well then, she would have to do it.

It wasn't going to be easy. Although he had gone, the taxi still seemed to be full of his dominating masculine presence. Karen felt an odd little shiver pass through her.

No, it wasn't going to be easy at all.

CHAPTER THREE

'WE'LL go straight to the hotel and book you in.'

Saul Marston dumped the last of the bags into the taxi and climbed in beside Karen. He leaned forward and tapped the driver, who had been slumped in his seat, his wide-brimmed hat pulled forward and an unlit cheroot sagging from his mouth. '*Lleveme a Hotel Fiesta Palace,*' Saul rapped out.

The driver sat up with a jerk and the cheroot dropped out of his mouth. '*Si, señor,*' he mumbled, starting up the noisy engine.

'They're inclined to go to sleep on you here if you don't watch 'em,' Saul remarked and Karen blinked stupidly. She herself had been floating in a half-sleep since Saul left her to find the luggage. As the taxi moved out into the swirl of traffic she tried to gather her wits together.

It was quite dark now and the moving lights of cars and buses reflected back from the faint smog that hung over everything. The screeching of brakes and revving of engines seemed to go right through Karen's head. 'I'm sure that isn't the name of the hotel where we're staying,' she said, rubbing her forehead confusedly. 'We were booked in at another one—I can't remember the name.'

'Ah yes, that was my secretary's doing. I cancelled your booking—it will be more convenient to have you at my hotel for tonight, especially as things have turned out. There are several matters I want to clear up before the conference. You'll be able to find all the papers in Ben Clark's luggage?'

'Oh yes.' Karen tried to sound like an efficient personal assistant, but she wished this awful muzziness in her head would go away.

'Good. I shan't be asking you for any technical information.' He shot her a quick sideways glance. 'Are you feeling O.K.?'

Nice of you to ask, she thought in disgust, I've only flown thousands of miles and had a traumatic shock and I'm worried out of my mind about Ben and about the whole situation. 'Yes, thank you, I'm feeling fine,' she said.

'H'm, well, you don't look it. You're probably hungry. I'll order an early dinner as soon as we get to our hotel—if we ever do,' he added as the taxi came to a squealing halt at red traffic lights.

'But—but I must go back to the hospital,' Karen said rather desperately. 'I must be there if Ben's having an operation tonight. He'll be feeling awful when he comes round, and if I'm there . . .'

'Look,' Saul said crisply. 'You're not going anywhere tonight, once we get to the hotel. We can keep in touch with the hospital by 'phone. They won't thank you for hanging about there, getting in the way.'

Karen leaned her head wearily against the back of the seat. 'Do you always push people around like this?'

'Not always.' There was a faint smile in his voice. 'Sometimes they push me around. Especially beautiful women,' he added, as the lights changed and the taxi started with an almighty jerk, throwing Karen sideways across the seat. Saul's arms were there to receive her and closed round her rather more tightly than was necessary.

The taxi rattled on, tangling with other cars, jockeying for position. 'It's a madhouse,' Karen muttered, disturbingly aware of the strong arm that was still holding her close.

'Agreed.' He drew her even closer. 'Allow me to offer protection. There, rest your head on my shoulder.' She heard a low chuckle from just above her ear. 'You see, sometimes the pushing around is mutual—due to the vagaries of the Mexican traffic system.'

There was no point in resisting, and anyway, in her present dazed state it was pleasant to lean against a man's strong body and feel the warmth of him through the thin stuff of his jacket. Hazily Karen was aware of his cheek pressing against the top of her head, of the fresh smell of his cologne. She felt her heart-beat quicken slightly, but only very slightly. Actually, she was too exhausted to respond to any sensual situation; all she wanted to do was to curl up and go to sleep. She supposed it was partly jet-lag, something she hadn't encountered before.

The hotel was of the super-deluxe variety, the entrance-hall the size of two tennis courts, the long reception counter lined with smiling clerks and buzzing with activity. Saul took charge of everything and Karen let him. It was a new experience for her to be looked after by a man as if she were a poor, weak female. She mustn't, she resolved, make a habit of it, but just now she was far too tired to bother about anything.

A smart Mexican bellboy carried Karen's luggage up in the lift with them and, when Saul opened a door on the second floor with his key, deposited the bags inside the room, accepted a tip with a huge grin, and departed, closing the door after him.

'Come in and sit down,' Saul said, waving towards a long, woven-cane sofa with brightly-patterned cushions. 'What'll you have to drink?' When Karen shook her head he poured her something into a glass and brought it over to her.

'This will keep you going until you get some food inside you.' He put the glass into her hand and went across to the telephone. She took a tiny sip of the brandy while Saul ordered a meal. She noticed absently that he spoke fluent Spanish, much too quick for her to understand. She looked around the room, which was comfortably furnished as a sitting room. There was a door on the far wall standing partly open, beyond which she could see a dressing table and the bottom end of a bed. Saul evidently had a suite here. He would, wouldn't he? He was rich enough to travel in luxury.

He came back from the telephone with his drink and sat down beside her. 'Shouldn't be long,' he said. 'I ordered steaks—that O.K. for you?'

'Yes, thank you,' murmured Karen. She was saying yes to this man far too often; she mustn't let it become a habit. She said, 'Perhaps I could go to my room before we eat?' She took another sip of the brandy and put the glass down.

'It's about four floors up—I'll take you up there later. Meanwhile, make free with my bathroom.' He spoke so casually that it would have seemed childish to argue and insist that she go to her own room. 'Thank you,' she said and picked up her travelling satchel from among her luggage and Ben's, which the boy had stacked beside the door.

The bathroom was all pale green, large and luxurious. It would have been lovely to have a shower but that would have to wait. She contented herself with washing hands and face. The blue denim suit she had travelled in had stood up fairly well to the strain, as had the white frilly blouse. Huge hazel eyes, heavy with weariness, looked back at her from the mirror over the wash-basin. She ran a comb through her dark hair and twisted it back into its knot flicking the straying tendrils over her ears and sighed as she thought again about Ben and what rotten luck he had had. How soon could they telephone to ask for news? Not yet, she supposed, it was less than an hour since they had left the hospital. Saul Marston was a bit casual about it all—she would have to insist on keeping up to date with news of Ben. And at the same time make sure that she looked after Ben's interests without in any way antagonising the man Saul. It was like walking along a knife-edge.

She returned to the sitting-room to find a waiter completing the setting of a table for dinner. Dishes with bulbous silver covers stood beside it on a trolley, and Saul was approving the wine. Karen hesitated for a moment in the doorway. She had taken it for granted that they would dine in the restaurant and this intimate little scene came as a faint shock. But she mustn't get silly and suspicious. Saul Marston didn't have any ulterior motive in bringing her to his private hotel suite, of course he didn't. It was purely business.

He looked round as she came into the room and smiled, and again that smile of his did something very peculiar to her inside. There was no doubt about it, he had what was known as a winning smile—when he cared to use it, which wasn't very often. 'Ah, there you are, Karen. Just timed it right.'

He nodded to the waiter, who put the bottle of red wine on the table with a flourish, pulled out a chair for Karen, served the food, and then retired with a bow.

At the sight and smell of the plump, juicy steaks with crisp sauté potatoes and petit pois, Karen felt quite faint with hunger. 'We won't waste time trying to make polite conversation just now,' Saul said. 'There are more important things to attend to. Eat up.'

She needed no further encouragement; she fell on

the food with zest. Saul kept her wine-glass topped
up; stacked the plates on the trolley as they became
empty; discovered a tempting array of pastries,
together with cheese and biscuits. And altogether
proved a courteous and thoughtful host.

Karen sighed as she crunched her final biscuit.
'That was lovely, what a pity it had to end. I really
have made a beast of myself, but my excuse is that I
haven't eaten for a long, long time.'

Saul carried the coffee-tray to a low table beside the
sofa and Karen poured out. 'I like to see a girl enjoy
her food,' he said, sitting down beside her. 'I find it
maddening to order a good meal and see my partner
picking at it like a scrawny sparrow.'

Karen giggled. 'I'd like to be a bit scrawnier myself
sometimes, but I enjoy my food too much.'

Saul lay back in his corner of the sofa, regarding her
lazily from under thick dark lashes. 'I'd say you're just
about right,' he said, his eyes resting finally on her
long, slender legs.

'You're an expert, I take it?' Heavens, what was she
thinking of, making a provocative remark like that?
She should be putting him down—pleasantly, of
course, but she didn't feel at her brightest and best at
the moment. Better get on with the business matters,
and then she could get to bed and sleep off this
drowsiness that was pulling at her eyelids. She got up
and went over to the pile of luggage, picking out Ben's
brief-case. 'I think everything you might want is in
here, Mr Marston,' she said. She carried it back to the
low table and, pushing aside the coffee tray, began to
spread out the contents of the case.

After a moment, when he didn't reply, she glanced
questioningly towards him and surprised an odd,
enigmatic look in his eyes. 'You're a very efficient
young lady, aren't you?' he said. 'And for God's sake

don't call me Mr Marston, it's bad for my self-image when a lovely woman calls me Mister. The name's Saul.'

He put down his coffee cup and moved along the sofa, nearer to her, picking up the top wad of notes. For perhaps a couple of minutes he studied them, turning the pages over, then he put them down again. 'I don't think I can concentrate tonight after all,' he said. 'I can think of better things to do.'

She turned her head and looked into his dark eyes and there was no mistaking the message in them. His arm went along the back of the sofa, pulling her gently against him.

She knew he was going to kiss her and that she should stop him. It might lead to all sorts of complications if she allowed him to think she was easy game. But she seemed to be enveloped in a kind of hazy cloud that made her limbs weak and her resolution even weaker. And when his mouth came down on hers the sensation was so delicious that she gave herself up to the almost hypnotic effect he was having on her. His mouth moved slowly against hers, teasing her lips apart gently. His hand stroked her cheek, her forehead, her neck, her arms, slowly, rhythmically. A warm languor claimed Karen, a feeling of utter content. She was yielding, passive, quite unable to resist anything that might happen.

What did happen was very strange indeed. One moment she was revelling dreamily in the sensuous pleasure of having her neck stroked. Then, quite suddenly, her eyelids drooped, her head went back against the sofa, and a black velvet darkness slid down over the room. Karen was asleep.

She wakened reluctantly, gradually forcing herself back to consciousness, her mind struggling to arrange itself into accustomed patterns, and failing. Everything was different.

She pulled herself up on to one elbow and looked around. The room was lit only by a single shaded wall-light and she was lying curled up on the cushioned sofa, covered by a warm duvet, still wearing the blue suit she had travelled in. Travelled—ah, that touched a chord! Then memory came flooding back like a tidal wave and she knew everything. She sat up, peering at her watch. It had stopped, and in any case it would be hours wrong because she hadn't adjusted it to the different time zone.

It must be early morning—faint streaks of light were showing round the edges of the velvet curtains. Ben! Karen thought with a cold pang of fear. What had happened—was the operation over—was he all right? She'd been going to telephone the hospital last night, and then—she'd fallen asleep. She'd let that man Saul kiss her and—what else? She couldn't remember. But all that faded into unimportance beyond the fact that even at this moment Ben might be—might be—

She had to find out what had happened—she just had to. Now.

She pushed back the duvet that covered her. Saul must have taken off her shoes before he tucked her up, because they were standing neatly beside the sofa. The thought of that man lifting her legs on to the sofa, taking off her shoes, covering her up, set up an odd kind of disturbance inside her. She pulled on her shoes jerkily and fastened the straps. It was all too— too intimate. Suddenly he had changed from the most casual business acquaintance, and one she disliked at that, to this almost domestic cosiness.

It wouldn't do, Karen told herself. She would establish them on a more businesslike course immediately. It was a pity that she would have to go into his bedroom and wake him up in order to do it, but she had to find out about Ben.

She found the light switch and the room was flooded with white light that made her blink. Going into the bathroom she swilled her face in cool water and felt more awake and ready to deal with the situation. Her thin white blouse had really lived up to its uncrushable label but the skirt of her suit was a wreck. She pulled it straight as well as she could and marched across the room into Saul's bedroom, the door of which was ajar.

The light from the adjoining room showed her his long body outlined beneath the bedclothes, one arm and shoulder thrust out carelessly. All of a sudden Karen felt very odd. She realised that she had never seen a man in bed before—except her father, and he wore pyjamas. She was pretty sure this man lying before her wore nothing at all. She stood there holding her breath, curiously reluctant to wake him, to touch him.

Then her heart gave a lurch as she saw, in the dim light, that his eyes were open, watching her. The brute—he hadn't been asleep at all, he had known that she was there.

She stood frozen to the spot. Then Saul's hand came out and before she could resist she was pulled down on to the bed beside him, his arm across her body, his other hand at her waist, so that she was quite helpless to move. He eased himself up on one elbow and his eyes glittered in the dim light that filtered through from the next room.

Karen stared up, like a small hypnotised creature before a great jungle cat moves in for the kill. 'W-what do you think you're doing?' she gasped idiotically.

'Isn't it obvious?' She heard the smile deep in his voice. 'Finishing what I began last night before you went to sleep on me. When a beautiful lady walks into my bedroom what do you expect me to do?'

'No—I can't—you mustn't——' her mouth opened to protest and he took full advantage of it, moulding his own mouth round hers in a way that sent tiny flames shooting down over her body. She was helpless to resist a kiss like that—not too brutal, not too sensuously arousing. Just pure ecstasy. When his hand went to her breast she shuddered and pressed her mouth deeper against his, and felt his arm move lower and lift her until she was pressed against his hard, strong form.

For a moment he held her there and in that moment Karen was lost to everything but the pleasure he was giving her. It was crazy madness but she wanted it to go on and on, and she couldn't have denied him anything he wanted.

Then, suddenly, he released her and rolled away with his back to her. He was breathing quickly and she knew that he had gone further than he intended and that now he was fighting for control. She swung her legs round and sat on the edge of the bed, and at last he turned and pulled himself into a sitting position and gave her a little push. 'Go away,' he said. 'Somewhere where I can't touch you.'

She slid off the bed and stumbled into a basket chair a few yards away. Her legs felt like stretched elastic.

They stared at each other in the half-light. 'Well,' he said at last. 'That got a bit out of hand didn't it?' She sighed with relief. Thank goodness! He was treating the whole thing lightly so she could too. 'Am I expected to apologise for going to sleep last night?' she said with a little laugh.

'For having jet-lag descend on you so abruptly? Of course not, it often does. It was a pity it had to hit you just when we were making progress though.'

Karen sat up straight. She had a feeling that the next few moments were critical, after what had just happened. She must strike exactly the right note now, establish a friendly but cool businesslike relationship between them, imply that a kiss was—just a kiss. Just an impulse born out of proximity, which was precisely what it was—for him. And for her? Dizzily she realised that never before had she been so aroused, so tinglingly aware of her own body.

She pushed the thought away. 'Why I came in to you just now was to ask the time—my watch isn't registering. I must 'phone the hospital for news of Ben, I'm very worried about him.' Now that she was regaining her sanity her anxiety took over completely, intensified by a horrible feeling of guilt. How could she possibly have behaved as she had just done and forgotten all about Ben? She felt dreadful. 'I must find out how he is. I meant to 'phone the hospital last night.' Her voice wobbled. 'Please, please do something about it.'

'Relax,' he said calmly. 'I 'phoned late last night myself. The op's over and he's O.K. We can visit any time after ten this morning. And the time now is——' he glanced at a travelling clock at the bedside '——just after seven.'

'Oh, spendid—marvellous. Oh, thank you.' That was a wonderful relief. Perhaps things were sorting themselves out at last.

'But of course,' Saul went on, 'after an operation like that he'll be in hospital for some days. No hope of his attending the conference I'm afraid.'

'No, I suppose not.' She felt suddenly quite hollow with disappointment. 'Does that mean that—that the possible deal is off?'

He leaned back against the pillows, watching her in the dim light. 'Would it matter so much to you?'

'Yes, it would,' she admitted. 'It would matter a lot. Ben's been through such a rotten time lately, and things have got pretty bad at the works. But you know that already, of course, that was why he approached you in the first instance. He was so hoping that—that somehow the company would be able to carry on. With your help,' she added, because that was what it amounted to.

'Yes,' he said thoughtfully. 'That's the situation from Ben Clark's point of view. But I asked you would it matter so much to you, personally.'

He was quizzing her again—trying to find out how much Ben meant to her. Well, she wasn't going to satisfy his curiosity. 'I should lose a good job,' she said flatly. 'That's always important.'

'O.K.,' he said, and his eyes glinted. '*Don't* tell me, I'll find out for myself.'

The man was impossible and she would dearly like to tell him so. She got to her feet stiffly. 'I'll find my room now, if you've got the key. I'd like a shower and a change of clothes.' She glanced with distaste at her crumpled skirt.

'It seems hardly worth while moving everything up,' Saul said. 'You be sorting out what you want while I have a shower and then the bathroom's all yours. We'll go down and have a working breakfast and discuss the various points I want to go over with you. And this time we really will discuss them,' he added with a wicked sideways glance at her. 'No sidetracking.'

She would have liked to come back with, 'Who started the sidetracking?' but it seemed wiser to leave the matter. Whatever happened she mustn't needle this man who held the future of Ben's company in his hands.

'O.K.,' she said, and when he seemed about to

throw back the duvet and get out of bed she beat a hasty retreat into the sitting room. Saul's mocking voice followed her. 'Don't tell me you're shy.'

As she unlocked her case she thought rather miserably that that was exactly what she was—shy. Well, perhaps not exactly shy, but certainly inexperienced in dealing with a man like this—a worldly, rich, sophisticated type, totally unlike any man she had encountered before. The difference was that with the boys she had dated up to now she had always felt that she could hold her own. She was careful never to allow an encounter to become too heated, or to seem to offer more than she was prepared to give. So far it had worked well and, truth to tell, she had never met a man to whom she had wanted to commit herself.

She had grown up with the rather pleasant feeling that she was a cool girl, not likely to be overwhelmed by a burning passion. She thought perhaps that her mother had helped her to form this image of herself. Her parents' marriage was typical of the sort of marriage Karen had expected, one day, to have herself—a marriage of shared interests, companionship, affection. She had never known them quarrel seriously about anything.

She opened her case and began to sort through its contents absently. If she married Ben eventually that was the sort of marriage she would have. She could give him so much that Christine had never given him—an interest in his work and help with it. Understanding. Love.

Love. Could she imagine herself feeling, with Ben, as she had felt just now, lying in Saul Marston's arms? Indulging in a brief, crazy, exchange of passion?

Oh, I don't know, she thought crossly, I just don't want to think about it now. From her dressing case she picked out bra, pants and sheer tights and a dress of uncrushable linen in a pale apple-green, with a matching short jacket. That was cool enough, it should give the right impression.

'Bathroom's all yours,' Saul's voice came from behind her and she turned to see him standing in the doorway, a blue towel knotted round his waist, his dark hair wet and gleaming. There was no doubt about it, he looked stunning. All superbly male, with his strongly muscled body, the dark mat of hair running down his chest, the width of his brown shoulders.

Karen was suddenly aware that she was staring at him and felt an unaccustomed heat rise to her face. 'Oh, yes, thanks,' she muttered, and hastily tossing the clean clothes she had selected over her arm she bolted past him into the bathroom.

Half an hour later she emerged. A leisurely shower and some time spent on hair and make-up had, she hoped, restored the image of the cool young personal assistant. Saul, too, was the picture of a successful executive, in a grey alpaca suit with a white silk shirt and royal blue tie. He was lounging back on the sofa studying a sheaf of papers. He looked up when she came into the room and then got to his feet, his eyes moving over her slowly.

'Wow!' he said appreciatively. 'I was going to complain about the time you were taking, but now I've seen the result it would be churlish. You look most delectable in that green thing—like one of those French apples. "Delicious" I think they're called.'

'Thank you,' said Karen composedly. He came across the room and put an arm round her shoulders and turned her towards the door. 'Breakfast,' he said. 'I'm starving.'

Beside the writing table was a cheval-glass hanging on a painted frame and Saul paused in front of it. 'We make a very fetching couple,' he said, tilting his head sideways with a grin. 'We could do great things together.'

Karen looked too, and in spite of herself she felt a small thrill as she surveyed their reflections side by side. A tall, goodlooking, impressive man. A slender, sleekly-groomed, dark girl beside him. That girl looked infinitely more poised and sophisticated than she was feeling.

But she mustn't give him a hint of that and as they walked on she said coolly, 'I'm ready to work as hard as you want, in any way I can, if it's to help Ben's interests.'

She was looking straight ahead as they went out to the lift, but she thought he smiled as he said. 'Thanks Karen, I'm sure you are. But I wasn't really thinking of Ben.'

Again Karen felt a jolt of something very near to fear. What did he mean—what did he want of her? She wasn't yet prepared to answer that question, or even think about it, but it nagged at the back of her mind as they had breakfast. The dining room was enormous and, as yet, sparsely occupied. They chose a continental breakfast and as they drank coffee and ate rolls and a delicious preserve made, so Saul told her, from pineapple and papaya, he began, at last, to talk of business matters.

'I've seen the books,' he said, 'but I need filling in on several matters.' He began to fire questions at her. What was the capacity of the workshop as it stood? Did they work to full capacity? What was the morale of the workers like? The absentee rate? What was the procedure for staff training? Had the company ever lost orders due to not meeting a delivery on date? Who attended to specifications? On and on until her head was spinning.

But she kept her wits about her and answered his questions as briefly and accurately as she could, and he nodded from time to time. She got the feeling that everything she said was being stored as data in a computer-like brain. 'The point is,' he said at last, leaning forward, his eyes holding hers keenly, that I think I might have a very good potential market for Ben Clark's stuff with several of the firms in our group. There'll be directors or representatives of all the companies in Acapulco for the conference and I'd like you to meet them.'

'Me?' Karen's voice rose a tone. 'But I shan't be coming to Acapulco now that Ben's in hospital here.'

'Oh, I think you must,' Saul said impassively. 'There must be a representative of Clark's there. It would look extremely bad if there weren't. I always make a point of keeping my directors informed of new plans and I should like to know I have their approval before I go ahead and finalise anything.'

'And if they don't approve?' ventured Karen.

Saul sat back and shrugged. 'Then we'll just have to think again, won't we?' he said smoothly and she knew she wouldn't get anything more definite out of him at the moment.

He said, 'You really *are* involved with Ben Clark's business, aren't you?'

'Yes, of course I am,' Karen said rather shortly. 'Ben's a grand person and I want him to succeed.'

He was silent for a moment, studying her face, then he said, 'You know, a girl like you shouldn't be acting as a nanny to a bloke like Ben Clark. Oh, a good chap, I grant you, and gifted too, but he isn't going to get anywhere under his own steam.'

Karen swallowed and prayed for strength to be able to take this without hitting back at him angrily. At that moment she disliked the man more than ever.

'I suppose it depends on where you want to go,' she said at last.

He looked surprised. 'But surely there's only one place. To the top of your particular tree. If you're out on a limb you're due to get shaken off. But don't let's argue about it. You want to go to the hospital, don't you, so let's make that our first priority. You can assure your Ben that his interests are being splendidly looked after by one very lovely and efficient personal assistant,' he added with a mocking edge to his voice.

Karen didn't condescend to answer.

At the hospital Saul sought out the doctor that Karen had seen the previous night. This morning he was helpful and affable, no hint of the patronising way he had treated her yesterday. She supposed that was the effect Saul had on people—or perhaps it was because Mexico was a man's country still, or so she had heard. Whatever the reason, she very quickly found herself taken by a young nurse into Ben's room.

She was a doctor's daughter; she didn't expect miracles. But even so she was horrified when she saw him lying there, so straight and still under the covers, his face ashen, all the life-saving apparatus of tubes and dials round his bed.

But he was awake, he knew her, he even managed a ghost of his usual grin. 'Ben—how are you? How are you feeling?'

'Fine,' he whispered, not moving his head. 'Just fine. They've—patched me up—O.K.'

She swallowed. 'You'll soon be feeling lots better. And when you get out of here it'll be a new beginning—I'm sure of it.'

She thought his eyes brightened a little. 'You mean—the company?'

She nodded eagerly. 'Yes. Listen, Ben dear. Saul Marston wants me to go to Acapulco, to the conference. He says there ought to be a Clark's representative there to be introduced to the directors of his other companies. Would you like me to go? I couldn't talk about the technical side of things, of course, it would only be to—well, just to be there, to keep the company's flag flying. What do you think? I hadn't planned on going, I hadn't even thought of it. I wanted to stay here, to be near you and come in each day and get you anything you wanted, but perhaps . . .' Her voice trailed off. Ben looked so dreadfully tired, it was a shame she had to come to him and ask about a thing like this.

'Just say yes or no, Ben. I'll do whatever you think best.' She took one of his cold hands in hers.

His eyes looked into hers in silence and she couldn't tell what he was thinking. Then he murmured, 'Yes, please go, Karen.' He drew in an uneven breath. 'And—look after yourself, my dear.'

'I will,' she promised. 'And perhaps I'll have some good news next time I see you.'

'Yes.' His voice was very faint now. Karen bent and kissed his forehead and turned away. It was then that she saw that the door was half open and Saul was standing there, looking in.

They walked away together in silence. Only when they reached the waiting taxi did Saul speak. 'Well?' he said.

Karen said chokily, 'He looks so terribly ill. I do hope he's going to be all right.'

Saul looked out of the taxi window. 'He's a lucky man to have a secretary who cares so much about his wellbeing.'

'Well, of course I care,' she said rather fiercely, and neither of them spoke again until they reached the hotel.

There were more papers to go through together. Saul was completely the businessman now, keen, abrupt, crackling with vitality as he went over point after point with her, delving into the most minute details of the working of the company. Karen thought she was holding her own—in fact she couldn't deny that there were some questions that she could answer perhaps better than Ben himself could have done.

Finally Saul closed the folders and stacked them together. 'I think that about ties it up for the moment,' he said. 'Now we'll have coffee and find out about the shuttle service to Acapulco. The rest of the gang will be arriving today and tomorrow we'll have our first meeting.'

Karen hesitated and then said, 'Before we have coffee do you think we could phone to the office in Lessington? I'd feel much happier if I could let them know what's happening.'

Saul consulted his watch. 'Good idea. We might just about catch them at the end of the afternoon if they're still there. I'll put a call through to Ward.'

He sat down on the bed and dialled, while Karen stood and waited. In no time at all, it seemed, he was saying, 'Ah—James—Saul here, in Mexico City. How goes it with you—still snowing? It is? Look, we've hit a bit of a snag here. Ben Clark's been taken ill and he's in hospital here in Mexico City. Karen—his P.A.—I don't think you've met her yet—is here with me and I think she'd like to have a word with——' he glanced at Karen. 'Who would you like to speak to?'

Karen thought quickly. 'To Charlie—or Jean.'

There was a pause and she could hear a man's voice at the other end of the line, talking to someone. Then Saul said, 'Yes. Yes, she's here, I'll put her on.' He held out the receiver to Karen. 'It's Jean,' he said. 'She was in the office when we rang.'

'Karen?' Jean's voice came clearly across the wire,

all those thousands of miles away and Karen had a vivid picture of her, in her blue boiler-suit, standing in the shabby office, with snow falling outside.

'Jean—I wanted you to know——'

Jean's voice interrupted, high-pitched, impatient. 'Yes, yes, Mr Ward's just told me—Ben's ill. Karen, what's the matter—how is he? Is it serious? What's *happening*?'

Karen sketched in the details briefly. 'He had the operation yesterday and he's come through very well, the doctors say. We went to the hospital this morning so that we could see Ben before we leave for Acapulco . . .'

'Before—*what*?' Jean's voice was three tones higher than usual.

'I'm going to Acapulco, for the conference,' Karen explained, and added, 'Ben asked me to.'

There was a moment's silence. Then Jean's voice again. She seemed to be speaking with difficulty, or else it was a very bad line. 'You're going away—and leaving him alone in hospital?'

'Yes, I have to, it's what Ben wants. He's being well looked after.' Another silence. 'Jean—Jean, are you there?' She shook her head and handed the receiver back to Saul. 'I think we've been cut off.'

But a moment later Saul was speaking to James Ward again, going over a few points of finance. Karen hardly listened. She went across and stared out of the window. Poor Jean, she'd had a shock. She thought a lot of Ben, in her reserved way. Karen wished she could have had more time to explain, to put Jean's mind at rest.

Saul had finished the call now. 'They seem to be getting along O.K.' he said. He rang for coffee and then checked that there was an afternoon flight to Acapulco. 'All set,' he said with satisfaction as a smiling dark-skinned waiter arrived with coffee on an elegant red-lacquered tray.

Karen poured coffee into tall mugs decorated in patterns of reds and yellows. 'Pretty,' she said, admiring them rather absently, still thinking about Jean. 'Cream?'

Saul shook his head. 'Black, please.' He sat back and held up his mug to examine. 'Yes, the Mexicans are great with pots. A lot of the stuff you see is from the villages but its all very cottage-industry. If they could step up production, hire assistants, they could raise their standard of living quite dramatically. As it is they can't produce the stuff in large enough quantities to make it economically viable.'

Karen looked at the dark, clever face of the man sitting opposite. 'Perhaps they like their life better as it is,' she said. 'Money isn't everything.'

He shrugged. 'It helps,' he said, and she knew the subject was closed.

Acapulco was all that Karen had heard and read about it—a perfect playground for the rich and famous. Golden sun, golden sands, tanned bodies skimming across the blue water on skis and sailboards or lying back behind the creamy bow-waves of speed-boats or lounging on the decks of luxury yachts. Their hotel towered above the bay, white as icing sugar against the dark green of hills and pale blue sky behind it.

Karen's room was on the sixth floor with a view across the bay and furnished with every possible detail that would make for comfort and convenience. A quick look round showed her a plump bed with a throw-over cover in the characteristic reds and yellows of an Aztec design. An easy chair stood near the long window. A white fitment ran all along one side of the room, with vanitory unit, T.V., writing desk, a small fridge. The other side of the room was lined with built-in cupboards and closets.

'You'll be O.K. here?' Saul followed the porter into the room without asking her permission. 'It was the best I could do at short notice—there aren't very many single rooms.'

'It's very impressive—every home comfort, in fact.' Karen walked across to the window and looked down across the greenery to the beach below, where a cluster of straw-thatched shelters nestled among the palm trees. 'Isn't this the room I was intended to have, then?'

'No. You and Ben were booked in at one of the other hotels. But now you're in my care I want you under my eye here.' He came up behind her and placed both his hands on the window-frame, and although he wasn't touching her she felt that his arms were round her and her breath caught in her throat.

'You don't have to look after me,' she said, keeping her eyes fixed on the scene below the window. 'I'm quite used to looking after myself. I'm twenty-three, you know. I've held down a job for five years and I speak enough Spanish to get by here. Please don't feel responsible for me.'

'A very pretty speech.' His voice was gently mocking. 'And I'm sure you're a very efficient young lady. Nevertheless, I've brought you here and I shall see you come to no harm. There will be a lot of males around at this conference, and most of them won't have brought their wives with them. You're a very lovely woman, Miss Karen Lane, as you well know, and the situation might have its hazards. I have a plan that will save us both quite a spot of possible trouble and embarrassment.'

'A plan?' She spun round then, and found her face only inches from his. When he didn't move she ducked under his arm and retreated to a safe spot in front of the row of clothes-closets. 'What plan?'

'I think,' Saul Marston said, turning round and in no way put out by her evasive action, 'that for the duration of the conference it would be as well if we allowed people to assume that you and I are—well—friends, if you get my meaning. Do you agree?'

'No,' Karen burst out hotly, forgetting that for Ben's sake she had to be careful not to antagonise this man. 'I certainly don't agree. I think it's a rotten idea.'

'Why?' he enquired lazily. 'Do you find me not to your taste?'

What a way of putting it! And why did he have to look so shatteringly attractive, lounging there with his hands in his pockets, smiling at her under those thick dark lashes of his?

'I don't find you anything,' she muttered crossly. 'I don't know you, Mr Marston.'

'Saul,' he said. 'Please.'

'All right then, Saul,' she said.

'And if not knowing me is the trouble,' he said. 'There's one very easy and enjoyable way of getting around that.'

She stepped back as he came towards her but she was standing against the sliding door of the closet and she could move no further. His hands came up and rested against the door, trapping her again, but this time she was facing him and there was no escape.

She looked into his face and he was smiling faintly and he was so close that she could see the tiny lines beside his dark, glittering eyes; the slight hollows beneath the high cheekbones; the firm mouth with more than a hint of sensuality about the lower lip. She watched his mouth come nearer and her inside stirred, almost in pain.

I can't deal with this, she thought wildly, I can't

resist him. None of her usual ploys to keep things from getting too intense seemed to work now. This emotion was something new and raw, something quite shattering.

Oh God, she thought, I'm going crazy, but more than anything in the world I want him to kiss me.

CHAPTER FOUR

DELIBERATELY he framed her face between his two hands and kissed her firmly on the mouth. Then his hands slipped down to her waist and for a fleeting moment he held her body hard against his. Karen had a wild urge to wind her arms round his neck, to draw him closer, to turn the brief kiss into a long, sensual delight. But before she had time either to resist the urge or give in to it he had released her and stepped away.

He smiled down into her bemused face. 'There,' he said, 'we already know each other a little better, and this could be by way of a prelude to—other things. But for now—duty calls. I expect the clans are gathering, ready for the "off" tomorrow. Shall we go down and join them? I'll see if my luggage has been brought up and come back here for you in five minutes. O.K.? By the way, my room is next door.' He grinned wickedly as he added, 'You can come and waken me again any time you like.'

'Oh you—you——' Karen exploded helplessly. It seemed to her that he was manipulating her just as he wanted. She might be a puppet on a string for all the initiative she was showing. She must assert herself now or he would imagine he could do anything he liked with her.

She turned away and went across to open one of her bags. 'I'll need more than five minutes,' she said crisply. 'A quarter of an hour at least. Oh, and before we meet anyone I want to find out where there's an Interflora agency in the hotel—there's bound to be

74

one, isn't there? I want particularly to order flowers to be sent to Ben.'

Saul walked to the door and opened it. 'Fifteen minutes then,' he said and added, with a lift of a dark brow. 'And of course we must send flowers to Ben, mustn't we?' He went out and shut the door.

Karen glared at the glossy white door. *We* indeed! Why should he want to associate his name with hers on the card that Ben would receive? She would make sure it didn't appear there. This gift was to be a purely personal matter, from her to Ben. How would Ben feel if he got a card signed Karen and Saul? Or, more likely, Saul and Karen? Would he feel hurt, or would he be pleased that she seemed to be establishing a good 'rapport' with the man who could save his company?

It was all so difficult, with Saul Marston behaving as he was doing. Why couldn't he have been middle-aged and happily married? It would be so much easier for her to carry out her responsibilities without having this—this intimate approach almost forced on her.

She opened her bags and began to hang up her clothes in one of the closets, looking at them doubtfully. Her mother had insisted on a shopping spree, but the pretty little cotton dresses they had chosen between them didn't seem quite right for what she had already seen of Acapulco. But after all, she reminded herself, she *was* here to attend a business conference. She slipped out of the linen suit and into a white sleeveless dress scattered with tiny blue forget-me-nots, belted in with a narrow blue sash. She sat down to tidy her hair and renew her make-up, leaning towards the pink-shaded mirror. Her lipstick had smudged when Saul had kissed her a few minutes ago; her hand was shaking as she wiped her lips clean with a tissue. Had he seen—had he guessed that she had wanted more than that one brief kiss? She must be very, very careful if it happened again.

Ben had said there was some woman Saul had been having an affair with who would probably be at the conference. If the woman were here, or soon to be here, then surely Saul wouldn't want to bother himself with her—Karen. That would be a relief, wouldn't it? That would be what she wanted? She tried to convince herself, but the heat that had risen through her body a few minutes ago was still burning inside her. She went across and dashed ice-cold water over her face and then concentrated on putting on her make-up all over again. By the time Saul tapped at her door and walked in she was smiling a cool, bright little smile that seemed to suit the role of an up-and-coming young woman executive.

Saul had discarded the shirt and jacket he had worn on the flight from Mexico City and was wearing a short-sleeved ivory-coloured sports shirt in a thin cotton material that showed off his firm arms and shoulders. She had to admit that he looked disturbingly attractive leaning against the door-frame, his dark eyes following her as she walked across the room to pick up her handbag. He was a picture of arrogant male self-satisfaction—the kind that most women are supposed to fall for. She could feel the tug of his masculinity reaching her, even across the room. She told herself that so long as she recognised the danger she would be armed to withstand it. She would just have to be very careful.

'You've been quick, and I must say the result is charming.' His voice was a deep drawl. 'Shall we go?'

Karen was sure she would never be able to find her way around the hotel alone. It was like a small city with all its corridors and restaurants and balconies and bars and lounges. Somewhere in the distance a guitar thrummed away and everywhere there were people sitting around in various stages of dress and undress under the palms, drinking, chatting, laughing. A smell of expensive perfumes and cigar-smoke hung on the air. Waiters in red uniforms with silver buttons padded around, silent-footed on the plushy carpets.

Saul led the way confidently through a shopping arcade with glittering jewellery and mouth-watering clothes behind plate-glass windows. 'You must have a browse around here before we go,' he said. 'Take back a memento of the occasion.'

'It all looks definitely out of my price range,' Karen said. 'Marks and Sparks is more in my line.'

Above her head she heard Saul chuckle and his hand closed on her arm. 'You must aim high,' he said. 'You won't always be a secretary, my girl.'

'Personal assistant,' she corrected him idiotically, because she couldn't think of anything else to say, and the touch of his hand on her arm was making her nerve-ends prickle.

'Sorry,' he smiled. 'Personal assistant. My remark goes for that too. You won't always be a personal assistant. I have other plans for you—tentative, of course, just at present.'

She wasn't going to ask him what he meant by that broad hint, and fortunately at the moment she spotted a florists and made straight for it, leaving Saul in the rear. She was conscious of him watching her as she stood in a bower of exotic colours and scents, making her choice of flowers, but he didn't attempt to interfere, or suggest that his name should be added to the card on which she scribbled her short message— 'Dear Ben—Get better soon—Love from Karen.' Her Spanish was just about equal to dealing with the salesgirl, and as she counted out the pesos on to the counter she felt quite pleased with herself for having coped with the small transaction efficiently. She gave Saul a cool smile as she joined him in the doorway.

'Happy now? Duty done?' he said with that hint of irony in his tone which he seemed to produce every time he spoke about Ben. She couldn't let that pass. 'It wasn't a duty at all,' she said coldly.

'Call it a labour of love then. Lucky Ben!' She saw the glint of amusement in his eyes and wanted to hit him, but managed to control her annoyance as they walked away down the wide passage and into a lift. She was going to have to exercise a good deal of control, one way and another, in the next few days, if Clark's Components was to survive.

When they reached the ground floor Saul led the way into a vast, ornate lounge, all red and black and gold and glittering glass and row upon row of multicoloured labelled bottles behind a horseshoe-shaped bar.

'Here we are,' he murmured, 'and the clans are gathering already as I expected. He raised a hand in salute to two men sitting on high stools at the bar. 'Well met, you two.' The two men stood up as Saul and Karen approached. 'Karen, Harry Walker—Max Friend. Max—Harry—Karen Lane. Karen's here representing Clark's Components of Lessington—you may have heard of the company,' he added smoothly. 'She's going to sit in on our deliberations and see how she likes us.'

'Well, well, that should brighten the proceedings somewhat.' Max Friend held her hand longer than was necessary and treated her to an unashamedly wolfish scrutiny. He was good-looking in a going-to-seed way, in white trousers and pink shirt. He had crinkly golden hair and bloodshot blue eyes that took in every bit of Karen at a glance.

The second man was a different type altogether—

thickset and square-jawed, with bushy eyebrows over steel-grey eyes—everyone's idea of a business tycoon, in his well-tailored lightweight suit. He took Karen's hand in a firm grip and eyed her keenly, glancing at Saul and then back again. Karen was perhaps oversensitive at the moment, but she felt sure he was deciding silently that she was probably Saul's girl-friend.

If he was, Saul was evidently not going to correct the impression. He ordered drinks and nodded towards a table. 'Let's be comfortable,' he said, and they all carried their drinks over and sat down. There was the usual exchange of small-talk about journeys—Max Friend had come from Florida, Harry Walker from Canada.

'So—we're all going after the exports, are we?' Saul remarked jovially, sitting back and sipping his drink. 'Good show. Is Liz with you, Harry?'

The big man shook his head. 'Coming on later, been staying with some people in New York.' Karen thought the glance he gave Saul was somehow guarded.

'Oh look who's here,' chortled Max, who was sitting next to Karen. He lowered his voice and leaned nearer to her. 'We are about to be joined by one of the seven wonders of the modern world.'

'What do you mean?' Karen said.

'A happily married couple, and if that isn't a wonder, what is? Mr and Mrs Lovey-Dovey.' He chuckled. 'They live in Wimbledon,' he added, as if that clinched the matter.

Several other men were joining them now and Saul was welcoming them, chatting to them. Chairs were pulled up, greetings were exchanged. Everyone obviously knew everyone else and the group began to take on the feeling of a business conference.

Harry Walker pulled his chair round and edged it in beside her. 'So you're from Lessington are you, Miss Lane? Pleasant place, I've been there once or twice on my way up North. Clark's Components, let's see——' he looked upwards, narrowing his eyes. 'No, it doesn't ring a bell I'm afraid.'

'We're quite small—at the moment,' Karen said guardedly. She had to be careful what she said here, certainly until she got her bearings.

'But hoping to be larger, eh?' The big man smiled rather tightly. 'It's all right, Miss Lane, we've all been in the same boat, needing a rescue operation at some time or other, Saul Marston being the rescuer, that's the way he operates. It's your own company, is it?'

'Oh no,' Karen said quickly. There was no need to be cautious about this. 'I'm only a stand-in for Ben Clark, my principal. Unfortunately he was taken ill on the flight and he's in hospital in Mexico City.'

'Ah—bad luck.' He took a puff at his cigar. 'Known Saul long, have you?'

'Only a couple of days. I hardly know him at all.' She must get that straight from the start, she thought, before Saul started giving everyone the wrong impression about their relationship.

'Ah,' said Harry Walker again, this time with a faintly knowing inflexion. Was it possible that Saul had *already* let it be thought that he and Karen were— she shied away from the current popular term—having an affair?

'Karen!' Saul's voice cut through the talk around the table. 'Come over here, darling, someone I want you to meet.'

The sound of his deep, velvety voice saying her name gave her a small flutter. But—*darling*! How dared he? She could feel Harry Walker eyeing her speculatively. She seethed with annoyance, but there was absolutely nothing she could do about it at this moment, with all these people around. It was appalling that Saul Marston should issue orders like that and she should have to obey tamely. On the other hand it would raise eyebrows if she behaved like a sulky wife or girlfriend. It would make the whole thing look too important. Then she saw that he was sitting next to the couple whom Max Friend had called Mr and Mrs Lovey-Dovey and she got up quickly, walked round the table, and hardly waited for Saul's introduction to the couple before she exclaimed enthusiastically, 'How lovely to meet you,' as if they were the two people in the world whose presence could make her hurry to obey Saul's command.

Saul pulled up a chair for her between himself and Mrs Goodall, who was a little dumpling of a woman with bright blue eyes and a page-boy haircut. Her fair straight fringe made her look rather like a cuddly doll, one of the old-fashioned kind, not a modern trendy one.

She covered Karen's hand with her own and squeezed it. 'How absolutely splendid to have another girl here! Usually poor little me has to amuse myself all on my own while these important men are doing their talking.'

Saul leaned forward. 'Too bad, Ann love,' he drawled. 'Karen's one of us, she's here to attend the conference.'

Mrs Goodall's mouth drew into a pout. She looked at Karen doubtfully. 'Are you really, my dear? You're not one of those feminists, are you?'

'Certainly not,' Saul answered for her. 'She's just a very bright business woman. And we won't leave you on your own too much, Annie. We'll have to arrange some excursions in our free time. You and Bill, Karen and I. How about that?'

'Oh yes!' Ann Goodall brightened. 'That will be lovely. D'you hear that, Bill? Saul's arranging a foursome for us, when you've finished your talking.'

Her husband turned back from the conversation he was having with the man on his other side and patted her hand. 'Splendid, my dear, splendid!' he said, and resumed his conversation.

Saul started to discuss U.S. markets with the man on his other side and Karen was effectively marooned with Ann Goodall, who proceeded to quizz her unmercifully. Who did she work for? How long had she been doing the job? Did she enjoy it, and was she terribly, terribly ambitious? Where did she live? With her parents? Oh, how nice, and what did her father do?

Karen answered mechanically, all the time conscious of Saul sitting next to her. The sound of his voice seemed to echo through her head and travel all down her body in a very peculiar way, although she could only catch a word here and there of what he was saying.

'Saul's a sweetie, isn't he?' giggled Ann. 'If I hadn't got my Bill I'm sure I'd fall for him myself. Not that he'd look at little me,' she sighed. 'He goes for glamour does Saul. Oh look, here's Harry's wife, isn't she *fabulous*? There's no other word.'

Karen turned to look and saw at once what Ann meant. Liz Walker had the kind of looks that could never be described as 'pretty'. She was fabulous, and that was all there was to it—tall, willowy, in an olive-green dress with long floating sleeves and a huge silver brooch at the lowest point of the V-neck—a point which was almost at her waistline. Her hair was a smooth, satiny russet showing in tendrils beneath an enormous black straw hat, and she had wonderful green eyes, heavily made-up so that she looked rather like a very beautiful snake.

The men were all on their feet as she joined the table, but she went straight to her husband and kissed him. Harry Walker's rugged face lit up; he looked like a small boy who has been given some longed-for birthday present. He pulled up a chair for his wife and she sank into it gracefully.

'I caught an early flight,' she said in a husky voice, looking round the table at the assembled group. 'Hullo, everyone, nice to see you all again.' Her glance stopped at Saul. 'Hullo, Mr Chairman.' She made a teasing moue of her lips. 'How's the great man?' Her eyes moved briefly to Karen, sitting beside him, seemed in one glance to dismiss her as negligible, and returned to Saul.

'Nicely, thank you,' Saul replied, in the same tone. 'How's yourself?'

'Exhausted.' Liz didn't look in the least exhausted. 'New York moves at a shattering pace.' She turned to her husband and laid a white hand against his cheek. 'Don't look so worried, my sweet. I'm not really exhausted. Actually I find New York marvellously stimulating. And business, I'm glad to say, was encouraging. I think they liked me—and my wares.'

'So they jolly well should,' Harry boomed, catching her hand and kissing it. It seemed to Karen an unlikely gesture from such a very unromantic-looking man. But you never could tell, could you? And he was obviously very much in love with his exquisite wife. 'Liz has started her own business recently.' He beamed proudly round the table. 'Costume jewellery.'

There was a hum of interest and congratulation from the assembled company, and then the talk became general again, and in a few minutes the party began to break up. The men drifted back to the bar, in twos and threes. Ann Goodall whispered to Karen, 'I simply must get my hair done. Liz always has that

effect on me, she makes me feel an absolute frump.
See you later, my dear. Come along, Bill.' She put her
arm through her husband's and led him away.

Saul said, 'Karen, I want you to meet Liz Walker.
You two should get on together.' He propelled her
across the lounge to where Liz and Harry had found a
small table to themselves. 'Liz, this is Karen Lane.
She's a stranger in our midst.'

Liz held out a languid hand and as Karen took it she
was conscious of a scrutiny from the green eyes that
held something a little more than a casual interest.
'Hullo, Karen, nice to welcome you to the talking-
shop. Harry tells me you're going to be part of the
proceedings, poor you. You work while we other spare
females lounge about acquiring a gorgeous tan.'

'I hope I'll have time to acquire a tan too,' Karen
said.

'I shall see to that,' Saul put in smoothly, draping a
possessive arm round Karen's shoulders. 'I intend to
organise Karen's spare time.'

'Oh yes?' Liz lifted perfect brows, and then, turning
to Karen she added lightly, 'You'd better watch this
man, Karen, he's dangerous.'

It was just ordinary social chit-chat, but something
in her voice, something in the look she exchanged with
Saul, something in the way Harry's eyes were fixed on
his lovely wife, seemed to ring a warning bell in
Karen's head. Saul knew the Walkers very well, that
was evident. Or was it just that he knew Liz Walker
very well? These were worldly, sophisticated people
and suddenly Karen felt very young and inexperienced.

Liz stretched and yawned. 'I need to relax,' she
said. 'And I must get out of my New York gear into
something more Acapulco.' She glanced round the bar
where all the women were wearing flimsy cover-ups

over their bikinis. Cover-ups which covered very little.
'I feel horribly overdressed.' Her eyes rested again on
Karen in her neat flower-sprigged shift and Karen felt
as if she were at a childrens' party. She really would
have to invest in some more appropriate clothes for
off-duty times. It appeared that beachwear was the
order of the day.

'You dining here?' Harry asked Saul a little
brusquely, and Saul shook his head. 'Not this evening.
I'm taking Karen off elsewhere—she needs a good deal
of briefing before tomorrow's meeting. She's being
very brave and taking on an understudy's part at short
notice. Harry will explain the circumstances to you,
Liz. See you.' He nodded amiably and led Karen
away, still with an arm around her shoulders.

In the lift he said, 'There's a restaurant I know
within walking distance where the food is excellent.
We'll make for that.'

Karen was beginning to feel hungry already but she
felt she should put up some sort of resistance to this
man's calm assumption that she would fall in with his
every wish. 'I'm not sure that I want to go out for
dinner,' she said, wishing that the lift didn't seem to
be enclosing the two of them in such intimate
proximity. Her pulses fluttered as her arm brushed
his. 'I'm rather tired.'

'Understandable,' he said smoothly. 'I suggest you
have a siesta first—most people do around sundown.
Nobody eats here much before eight. We'll meet down
in the same bar at seven-thirty. Think you can find
your way?' They got out of the lift and he walked with
her to the door of her room.

It was no use arguing with him—she always lost. 'I
expect so,' she replied rather shortly and went in and
closed the door'.

She took off her dress and lay down on the bed. It

would be wise to snatch a short sleep, but in spite of the broken night she had had last night, sleep had never seemed further away. As she tried to relax she kept remembering last night and the way it had finished, remembering the way Saul had pulled her down on to the bed beside him, remembering his kisses. Her cheeks began to burn and the glow spread lower and lower until her whole body was encompassed.

This wouldn't do at all, she scolded herself, allowing that man to excite her like this—more than any man had done before. But of course, she told herself, he was the expert. Everything he did would be calculated, practised, making love just as much as making money. The thought left her feeling weak. What did she know about a man like Saul Marston? He lived in a different world from the one she had lived in until now. A jet-setting, international world where people played by different rules from those of the small-town circles she was accustomed to. And somehow she had to try to adapt, for Ben's sake, to hold her own in the conference room—and out of it. It was the latter prospect that filled her with the greatest alarm. She didn't know what Saul intended, but she could hazard a shrewd guess. He intended to get her into his bed, he'd made no secret of that. She would be an amusement, a spare-time diversion, for the days of the conference. Or rather, the nights.

She got up and walked over to the window. In the cool, air-conditioned room she was shivering and she pulled a wrap round her as she stood looking out at the scene below. The sun had set and the sky was streaked with magnificent colours—flames and greens and golds that merged down into the waters of the bay, providing a picture of breath-taking beauty. For a minute or two Karen watched, spell-bound, forgetting everything except the wonder spread out before her. Then, almost before she realised what was happening, the colours faded and the darkness took over with tropical suddenness. The sky changed to misty grey and quickly to velvet black, and then it was the myriad lights from the hotels that glittered against the darkness and reflected in the gently-moving water.

Karen drew in a long, sighing breath. If only Ben could be here to share the magic of this place with her! Perhaps she would find she was in love with him and then Saul Marston would have no place in her life. Everything would be so simple, whereas as it was everything was so complicated.

Somehow she had to avoid antagonising Saul until he had made up his mind about Ben's company. But surely that didn't include sleeping with him? He wouldn't make that a kind of condition? That would amount to blackmail and she was fairly sure that Saul wasn't the kind of man to let his business judgment be clouded by personal considerations. If he wanted to take over Clark's Components he would do so whether or not she was willing to cheapen herself in the process.

This was wild thinking. And it became even wilder as she asked herself how Ben would view the possibility of exchanging the continuing life of his company for his personal assistant's honour. Karen giggled rather hysterically. It sounded like the plot of a Victorian melodrama. She drew the curtains and switched on the light. Guessing what might happen would get her nowhere, she would just have to play it by ear.

She went over to the closet and selected a dress to wear—something that would underline her role in this situation. Certainly nothing even vaguely provocative. Two dresses for evenings, her mother had said. One was a slinky ivory satin with a huge ruffle round the halter neck and almost no back. It was a fun dress and Karen loved it—but not tonight. Oh no, definitely not tonight. She took the second one off its hanger. This was much more suitable—a midnight blue organza with long full sleeves and tiny buttons up the front, from the waist to the demure frilled neckline that gave her face a hint of playfulness to contrast with its serious expression. This evening she must underline the seriousness and forget the playfulness.

She twisted her hair into a French knot, and kept the hanging tendrils to a minimum. She spent time over her make-up, keeping it muted and subtle. Misty blue eye-shadow, a tender pink lip-gloss, a hint of foundation to tone down the colour in her cheeks and remove the impression that she was anticipating the evening with excitement. She certainly wasn't, she assured herself. What looked like excitement in the colour of her cheeks and the sparkle in her hazel eyes was nothing more than the light of battle. She was going to hold her own against a formidable opponent.

She glanced at her watch. Seven-thirty, he had said and it wasn't yet seven. But she felt too restless to sit here in her room. She tossed a lacy black shawl over her arm and took the lift down to the ground floor. Quiet hung over the big rooms that had lately been buzzing with talk and laughter. Evidently Saul was right—people didn't emerge for dinner until some unearthly hour like eight or nine o'clock.

Karen felt quite hollow inside; she would pass out with hunger if she had to wait another two hours. She looked round for a snack-bar or some such and eventually strolled into a small side bar that was offering freshly-made fruit drinks with tempting bowls of delicious chewy little cakes of fruits and nuts like nothing that Karen had ever tasted before. She ordered a drink of lime with tiny strawberries floating in it and was eating her third cake when she was aware that someone had slid on to the high stool beside her. It was Max Friend, looking like a heart-throb from a very old film, with his corrugated gold hair and his world-weary expression.

'Hullo, sweetness, all on your own?' He turned faintly bloodshot blue eyes on her. 'Drinking alone isn't allowed, you know.'

Karen raised her eyebrows. 'As it's only fruit juice it doesn't count,' she said coolly. She didn't like the man much and would have normally given him a brush-off in no uncertain manner, but she hesitated. She had no idea how he ranked in Saul's group of companies and it would be stupid to start off by making enemies.

He eyed the tall glass of green liquid. '*Only* fruit juice? Oh, we'll soon change that.' He beckoned to the barman and indicated by gestures and speaking loudly in English that he wished a gin to be added to Karen's glass.

The barman gave him a straight look and gabbled a reply. As Max looked flummoxed Karen put in under her breath, 'I think he's telling you that this bar only sells fruit drinks. That,' she added pointedly, 'is why I came here. I wanted a fruit drink.'

'Oh.' Max Friend had the grace to look slightly apologetic. 'I see I've been put in my place.'

'Not at all,' Karen said with the faintest of smiles at his discomfiture.

Max laughed. 'Well, obviously this is no place for little me. Anyway, I've probably had enough booze for the present.' He leaned towards her confidentially. 'That's the worst of these get-togethers—you have to be sociable and have a drink with everyone and before you know where you are you're one over the eight.'

'Only one?' Karen murmured.

'We-ell, maybe three or four,' he grinned ruefully. 'Look, let's go down to take a look at the Pacific Ocean, that should blow the cobwebs away.'

Karen hesitated. There was still twenty minutes to go to half-past seven, and she didn't want to admit that she was waiting for Saul. Besides, it would be nice to walk down to the water. 'O.K.' she agreed.

The sand was still warm from all the daylight hours of sunshine. The sea was calm and tiny waves broke lazily at their feet as they stood on the edge of the tide. Myriad dots of light from the soaring hotel buildings pierced the darkness of the sky and at the far end of the bay a full moon was floating like a white balloon.

'It's almost too perfect to be real,' Karen said. 'You begin to think you're looking at a stage backdrop.'

'A backdrop for a very lovely lady,' Max murmured. Slipping an arm round her waist, he crooned, 'Moonlight becomes you, it goes with your hair.'

Karen wriggled away. 'My hair's dark, hadn't you noticed?'

'Of course I've noticed. I've noticed every little thing about you, darling, since the first moment you walked into the bar with Marston. I thought, God, this is a bonus. Something to take a chap's mind off his troubles.'

She took the opportunity to change the subject. 'So you've got troubles,' she said lightly. 'Haven't we all?'

He stared out across the expanse of gently-heaving glassy water. 'Divorce pending,' he said gloomily.

Oh goodness, another of them! What could she say to him? Bad luck, try again, like one of those computer games. Karen was silent, which she soon realised was a mistake because Max began pouring out his sorry story. All *she* wanted was to get her own back, he grumbled. *She* was grabbing everything, the house, the furniture. Putting in a ridiculous claim for the childrens' education. He was going to be broke, he didn't know how he could carry on.

Karen was remembering Ben and *his* divorce, and how he had never said a word against Christine, though goodness knows he would have been entitled to. But Max Friend was another sort of man altogether. He was getting almost maudlin now, probably partly the result of all the drink he had inside him.

'You can't imagine what it's like to meet a girl like you, sweetheart.' His arm crept round her again. 'A lovely, warm, sympathetic girl.'

But I haven't said a word, Karen thought, half amused, half pitying. The poor wretch was in such a state she hadn't the heart to disengage herself.

She didn't have to. From behind them a hand plucked Max Friend's arm away from her waist none too gently and Saul's voice said, 'That'll do, chum. This is my territory. Keep off in future, will you?'

Max turned, staggering a little, his mouth gaping open foolishly. 'Oh, it's you, Saul.' He giggled. 'Sorry and all that, I didn't know.'

'Well, now you do,' Saul said shortly. He turned to Karen. 'Are you ready? Come along then, we'll walk.' He took her arm and, leaving Max standing where he was, propelled her up the beach.

On firm ground Karen stopped. 'Wait a minute, I've got sand in my shoes.' She pulled off one of her black patent sandals and shook the powdery sand out on to the tarmac. Standing on one foot to replace the sandal she tottered and clutched at Saul's arm to steady herself. It felt like a rock—a rock that was somehow shot through and through with magnetism which vibrated along her nerves. 'S-sorry,' she murmured unsteadily and he laughed. 'Don't hurry,' he said amusedly. 'I'm enjoying it. Now do the other one.'

When she had finished Karen let go of his supporting arm quickly, and they walked along side by side beneath the palm trees, not touching.

'You see?' he said. 'I warned you, didn't I?'

'Did you?' She pretended not to understand.

'About the big bad wolves that would be attending the conference. Not that Max Friend is a very big wolf. Just big enough to be irritating.'

That was Karen's opinion too, but she said, 'He seems quite harmless. He was merely telling me about his divorce.'

'And you were doling out sympathy, I suppose. A lovely, warm, sympathetic girl!' He imitated Max's slurred tones unkindly.

'As a matter of fact I wasn't,' Karen said. 'Although if you hadn't barged in when you did I might have done. I'd be sorry for anyone with a broken marriage.'

Saul's chuckle was ironic. 'I,' he said, 'would be sorry for anyone with a marriage—period.'

'You're not married yourself?' Karen said and suddenly his answer seemed vitally important.

'Me? Married? Never in this world. You only have to look around you to see where *that* road leads.'

'You wouldn't want children—a son to carry on the Marston empire?' she said innocently.

He lowered his head and she looked up and met his gaze. His face was in shadow but in the twinkle of lights along the waterfront his eyes were glittering dangerously. 'Don't you try taking the mickey out of me, Miss Karen Lane,' he murmured. 'I have my own ways of dealing with females who issue a challenge.'

A tremor ran through her. The words were light but there seemed to her heightened awareness to be a thread of menace running through them. 'I'll remember that,' she said, and her voice shook a trifle.

'Mind you do,' he growled, and as they walked along together the space between their two bodies seemed to be sparking and crackling with electricity. Karen's mouth was dry and her hands were clenched. It was as if she was being pulled against her will towards the man beside her by some invisible, irresistible force of nature.

She didn't know whether she actually moved or whether he did. All she knew was that the next moment his arm was holding her strongly against him and in the shadowy darkness his mouth found hers in a kiss that sent thrill after thrill coursing down her body. When he let her go she swayed like a rag doll and would have fallen if his arm had not still been holding her.

He looked down into her eyes and the light filtering through the palm trees fell on his face. His expression was no longer ironic or teasing. His face reflected the same hunger that she felt inside herself. 'It seems we do something to each other, doesn't it?' he said, very low.

Karen drew in a deep breath. 'Nothing that we can't cope with, I'm sure.' She was pleased with the comparative steadiness of her voice. 'Moonlight in Acapulco no doubt plays all sorts of tricks with one's emotions. We needn't take it too seriously.'

He held her a little way away. 'What are you afraid of, Karen?' he said.

'I'm not afraid.'

'Then why are you trembling?' he said.

'I just told you.' She managed a smile somehow, she never knew how. 'Moonlight in Acapulco. It goes to one's head.'

He laughed, a deep laugh that reverberated all

through her. 'Not to the head, little Karen. The head doesn't come into it at all.'

She was getting control of herself now. 'Well, mine does,' she said shortly. 'My head tells me that I must control my behaviour.'

He linked his arm through hers and they walked on. 'Why?' he said at last, after a silence. 'Is it Ben? Or someone else?'

There wasn't time to weigh up her answer. She only knew that she must at all costs protect herself from falling into a veritible abyss of love for this man beside her.

'Ben has asked me to marry him,' she said rather baldly.

'Oh, I see.' His voice was soft, thoughtful. 'And may I know what your reply was?'

'No,' she said. 'You may not. Nothing is settled yet. But——' suddenly her voice changed, her words seemed to run away with her '——but don't you see, I can't—*can't*—start anything with you, or anyone else while Ben's lying there in hospital. So I'll be grateful if you'll—you'll stop behaving as if you . . .'

'Wanted you?' he said amusedly. 'But I do, you know. I want you very much, more than any woman I've met for a long, long time. I've wanted you since the moment I set eyes on you in that crumby little office in Lessington. And I'm certainly not as noble as you are—it's Ben's bad luck that he can't be on the scene but unless his ring is on your finger then I don't consider you—er—out of bounds, so to speak.'

'Oh!' Karen couldn't speak, she was almost in tears—tears of frustration and confusion. She tried to draw away but he held her arm tightly in his grip as they walked along. It was ridiculous, strolling along in this perfect spot under the palm trees in the moonlight discussing whether or not Saul would make love to her as if they were talking about the weather, or the scenery. Or was this the usual way that people behaved in his world?

He stopped and she stopped with him. 'This is our restaurant,' he said. 'And I suggest we postpone the argument until later and just enjoy the good food. Agreed?'

She swallowed. 'I don't want to argue with you,' she said, and realised a moment too late how that sounded, when he laughed and said, 'Fine! That's what I wanted to hear. Now come along and meet my friend Carlos. He'll fall in love with you too, I promise you.'

He was so—so smooth and urbane and utterly maddening. She would have loved to reach up and hit him—hard. Hit that ironic grin off his handsome face. But that would be over-reacting, wouldn't it? She must just try to play the whole thing as cool as he was doing.

But as she followed him into the restaurant she felt as if she were following him into jungle country that was strange, frightening, and yet breathlessly, tinglingly alive.

CHAPTER FIVE

'Outside or inside?' Saul said as they climbed the steps. 'The inside's small but it's air-conditioned. Most of the action's on the outside deck though, and it shouldn't be too warm outside this evening.'

Karen thought quickly. The outside sounded less intimate. 'Oh, outside then, please.'

A small man with a brown face and a huge moustache hurried towards them. 'Señor Marston. 'Ow are you? It is good to meet again.'

'Good to be here, Carlos. I've been away far too long. Have you got a table for us?'

Carlos beamed. 'For you, señor, the best table in my restaurant.' He led them proudly to a side table where a tall, whispering tree overhung the deck, and pulled out a chair for Karen with a flourish. 'The señorita will be 'appy here?'

'The señorita will be enchanted,' Saul said drily, with a sideways glance at Karen. And as Carlos hurried away to give the order for aperitifs Saul smiled into her eyes as he sat down close to her at the small table. 'Even if you aren't enchanted you are certainly enchanting,' he remarked. 'I like that dress very much.' He leaned towards her and took the black lace shawl from her shoulders and Karen had to resist a quite mad urge to move nearer so that their bodies touched. Stop it, she almost shrieked at herself inwardly. Just *stop* it.

'Yes, it's very clever,' Saul went on musingly, his gaze fastened upon the tiny buttons that ran up the front of the bodice. He touched one of them with a long, brown finger. 'These simply ask to be unfastened.'

She smiled a cool little smile as their eyes met, but how she did it she didn't know. 'Oh dear, and I chose this dress because it looked suitably chaste for a business dinner,' she said. She almost laughed with satisfaction; she was getting the hang of this sort of exchange now. It meant nothing at all.

His brows went up whimsically. 'Are you, Karen?'

'Am I what?' she said, before she had time to think.

'Chaste,' he said with a tiny shrug.

She caught her breath. 'I thought you brought me out to talk business,' she said.

He leaned back, eyeing her lazily. 'You couldn't talk business in surroundings like this, now could you?' He waved a hand towards the dark, mysterious stretch of sea, lit at the verges by the lights from the waterfront; at the lush greenery beneath and around them, running down to the water; at the round white globe of the moon sailing serenely above. 'Now, could you?' he pleaded.

Karen's lip twitched. 'Perhaps not. Neither is it the place for a much-too-personal grilling either.'

'I just like to get things straight at the beginning,' he said suavely. 'But no matter, the truth will doubtless emerge in due course.'

A waiter arriving for their order, and another waiter with drinks spared her the necessity of finding an answer to that. It was very exhausting, trying to hold her own conversationally with a man like Saul Marston, Karen thought as she hid her face behind the huge menu card.

'What do you fancy?' Saul enquired. 'American or Mexican? Carlos can provide an excellent steak or if you're feeling more adventurous I'd recommend a beef enchilada.'

'I'll be adventurous,' Karen said. 'Just so long as it's not too hot.'

'I can promise you that Carlos will serve it just as you like. Mexican food doesn't have to be fiery—although it can be. But we mustn't burn you up—you'll be needed for the meeting tomorrow.'

Ah, thought Karen, business at last! When the waiter had departed she said, 'You told Mr Walker that you wanted to brief me for tomorrow's meeting.'

Saul gave her a lazy smile over the rim of his wineglass. 'That was just an excuse to get away from Harry and Liz, I didn't fancy spending the evening as a foursome.'

'She's very beautiful, isn't she?' Karen said, watching his face.

'Very,' he agreed drily.

'Have they been married long?'

He smothered a yawn. 'A couple of months, I believe. Now, let's change the subject, shall we? Tell me about you, that's far more interesting.'

'More grilling?'

He sighed. 'That's a harsh way of putting it. I'm interested—I want to know all about you. About your parents—where you live—where you went to school—what you do in your spare time—what sort of books you like—music—pictures—films . . .'

She thought, Oh, and I want to know everything about you too, but not for the same reason. You're just making polite conversation, whereas I . . .' She checked herself here. You couldn't fall in love with a man in just two days, not counting that time back in the office in Lessington, when she'd hated him on sight. You couldn't, of course you couldn't.

'Go on—talk,' he said, smiling at her.

She looked at him doubtfully, and then a strange thing happened. For a moment the people at the other tables disappeared and there was only Saul, leaning back in his chair, watching her out of those lazy dark eyes of his. There was only the distant sound of the waves lapping on the beach, and the faint rustle of the trees and the pungent scents of unknown flowers drifting on the warm, moist air.

Karen blinked and swallowed. 'My parents are both doctors,' she began woodenly, 'and I live at home. I went to school at the local comprehensive. Do you want to hear how many O-levels I got?'

He was laughing silently. 'Relax, darling,' he said, Then he pushed back his chair. 'Look—will you excuse me for a few minutes—I've got a 'phone call I want to put through.'

She watched him walk away and tried to concentrate on the diners at the other tables but was only conscious of the general air of luxurious, almost voluptuous enjoyment that hung over the whole place. In the light from the slung red lanterns the men all looked dashing and handsome—white teeth flashing against brown skin; the women all creamed and scented and smoothed, gorgeous in their daringly cut-away gowns. The smell of their perfumes mingled with the aroma of well-cooked food. There was a murmur of conversation, punctuated by low bursts of laughter. Waiters hovered, corks popped. It would be so easy to sink into this expensive world of ease and luxury. Karen wondered if it was still snowing back in Lessington and that thought brought her back to a degree of sanity.

Saul returned and slipped into his chair. 'I rang up the hospital,' he said. 'It seems that Ben's condition is still satisfactory.'

Karen had a sharp stab of guilt as she realised she hadn't even thought of Ben since she left the hotel. 'Oh, that was kind of you,' she said hastily. 'Thank you so much.'

Saul smiled. 'I admit to a certain amount of self-interest,' he said. 'Now you can relax and enjoy your dinner.'

Ah—he had thought that her stiffness had been due to worrying about Ben. Well, at least she hadn't given herself away, that was something to be thankful for. And she certainly intended to enjoy her dinner.

There was no more questioning. Saul put himself out to entertain her during dinner. Mexico was evidently one of his favourite places and he told her fascinating snippets of its history and cultures, of its mountains and jungles, and volcanoes, of all the civilisations that had laid layer upon layer of their own colourful, exotic patterns on its cities and villages. Karen found herself the one to ask questions now.

'How come you know Mexico so well?' she said. 'Have you ever lived here?'

He shook his head. 'But my grandfather was of pure Indian stock,' he said. 'He married an American and their son—my father—visited England and married my mother there. I'm a bit of a mongrel, but I'm proud of my heritage and I've been back often to poke about in the old villages. Many of them have hardly entered the twentieth century yet.'

She looked at his dark face, the skin taut over high cheekbones, the arrogant nose and haughty mouth. 'That explains a lot about you,' he said, her eyes dancing. 'I can just picture you as an Aztec chief, all decked out in gold and precious stones, being macho and autocratic and assuming you can take whatever you want.'

He put down his glass and his hand closed over her wrist painfully. 'Watch it, my girl,' he said, 'or I'll give you a demonstration here and now.'

She tried to shake his hand off, without success. 'You're hurting me,' she gasped. 'Let me go.' She glanced round the other tables, but nobody was taking the slightest notice.

'I can wait,' he said and released her wrist.

Karen rubbed it. The man was a savage. So much for having a light conversation with him. She wouldn't relax again, she vowed, she'd be on her guard with every single thing she said.

A group of musicians had come in and were settling down with their instruments behind a screen of green twining leaves and soon the haunting music of guitars was thrumming through the warm evening air. Then the dancers took the space in the centre of the deck— two girls and two men in Mexican costume—and as they whirled and stamped and clapped, the temperature around seemed to rise with the mounting rhythm of the music. Karen could feel the throb of excitement taking hold of her and when the dance finally ended she joined in the sigh that went round the tables before the applause broke out.

'Powerful stuff,' Saul said, very low, close to her ear. 'Authentic, too.'

'It was wonderful.' Karen was unaware that her cheeks were flushed, her eyes brilliant. 'It's one thing to see it on TV, but quite another to see it live.'

His eyes were locked on hers and she was totally unable to look away. At last he said softly. 'Shall we dance?' as a few couples took the floor. She stood up and slid into his arms. The band was thrumming a slow, smootchy tune now and Saul rested his cheek against Karen's hair and they swayed together in and out of the pools of light cast by the lanterns. His arm circled her waist so closely that she felt they were one body and that was how she wanted it, she thought hazily. He lowered his head and placed his lips against her forehead, just above her ear, and let them rest there as they danced and Karen was conscious of a strong stirring inside. She felt warm and soft and fragile, as if the man who was holding her could crush her with one hand if he wanted to. Her arm went up round his neck, pressing him even closer and she wanted the music never to stop.

But finally it did and as they returned to their table Saul said huskily, 'Shall we go?'

They wandered back towards the hotel in the moonlight, and when Saul's arm went round her her own hand crept round his waist and they sauntered along, linked together, not speaking, the scented air enclosing them like a warm veil. Karen had ceased to think what would happen when they reached the hotel, ceased even to care. This was a magical night. Nothing was quite real and even the man beside her seemed to have taken on a kind of magic. Like a god, she thought, giggling a little. Like one of those old Aztec gods, maybe. She knew she had drunk too much of the local wine with dinner but she didn't care. She didn't care about anything.

Just before they reached the hotel Saul drew her into the shadows and pulled her against him. Then, slowly, he kissed her and it seemed the most natural, inevitable thing in the world that she should reach up and lock her arms round his neck and bury her fingers in the crisp hair at the back of his neck and kiss him back. When he finally let her go it was with a quick intake of breath. 'Not here,' he said, very low. 'There are better places.'

She was in a kind of dream as they entered the hotel and walked towards the lifts, scarcely aware of the people around, until a man's voice called, 'Ah, Saul, here you are at last, I've been watching out for you.

Karen blinked and saw the heavily-built figure of Harry Walker coming towards them. She heard Saul mutter some unrepeatable word under his breath, but probably Harry didn't hear it because he was barring their way into the lift and talking at the same time. 'It's Ferguson,' he was explaining worriedly. 'I knew you'd want to know at once because his new company extension is on the agenda for tomorrow.'

Saul moved impatiently. '*What* about Ferguson?' he rapped out. 'What's he been up to now?'

Harry Walker ran a finger round his collar. He was the only man in sight wearing a collar and tie. 'There was a 'phone call for you but you weren't to be found so I took it. It seems Ferguson has got himself into some sort of jam and he's landed in jail.'

'Here in Acapulco?' Saul rapped out.

Harry James nodded. 'He's asking for you to go— and bail him out, I suppose.'

'Hell!' exploded Saul. 'I've a good mind to let him stew.' He was silent for a moment, his face dark and angry. Then he shrugged. 'O.K. I suppose I'll have to go and see what it's all about.' He turned to Karen. 'Sorry, darling,' he said. 'I'll have to leave you on your own for a bit.'

The magic had gone. The spell was broken. 'Of course,' she said, walking past Harry to the lift.

Saul hesitated. 'Karen, I——' He looked doubtfully at her. Then, with a frustrated little shake of his head he strode off across the lobby with Harry Walker, who was almost panting to keep up with him.

Up in her room Karen sat on the bed, her heart thudding. She felt as if she had passed through some overwhelming crisis, and in a way she had. She'd passed through it and come out on the other side unscathed—but through no decision of her own. If Saul hadn't been called away she would have been in his room now, in his arms, probably in his bed.

She shuddered and got up and locked the door. She had a second chance and now she knew what she must do. When you were in mortal danger you stopped and fought—or you ran away. Tonight had proved that fighting with Saul could only end one way. It wasn't fair but there it was, and to let him make love to her would be a wild, ecstatic madness that would last for—how long? A few days, the length of time they were in Acapulco. And after that—what? How could she face Ben, how could she tell him she loved him and would marry him when all her body was shaken with memories of another man?

There was only one sane way and that was to avoid being alone with Saul. It shouldn't be impossible, there were plenty of people around. Tomorrow would be given over to meetings and from tomorrow on her dealing with Saul must be on a business basis and nothing more. If necessary she would tell him straight out that she was going to marry Ben.

As she got undressed and into bed she made herself think of Ben and a tenderness and affection gradually took the place of that wild madness she had felt with Saul. She began to plan for her life with Ben. They would sell Ben's house, where he had lived with Christine, and buy a cottage in one of the outlying villages perhaps. She could still work with him—until the children came along. She could make him so happy; make up for all the misery and loneliness he had suffered. And even if Saul didn't take Clark's into his group there must be another way that Ben could succeed, with her help. She could give him confidence in himself so that he could start again—

She began to get drowsy, drifting between sleeping and waking. She must get a good night's sleep tonight and be ready for tomorrow. There might be something she could do for Ben and for Clark's tomorrow at the meeting; she must be rested and fresh to tackle anything that turned up. Must—think—about Ben—

Suddenly her eyes flew open wide. There was a faint noise as if the handle of the door were being turned cautiously and Karen froze, lifting herself on one elbow, staring into the darkness. 'Karen.' Saul's voice came from the other side of the door, very low, and when she didn't answer after a moment or two, he said again, 'Karen, it's me, are you awake?'

She held herself still, every nerve quivering, every muscle taut, and after what seemed an age she heard a door close further down the corridor. Saul had given it up.

She sank back on the bed and pulled the duvet over her head, laughing and crying at the same time. She had won a battle with Saul—with herself. But she felt horribly like a loser.

Karen was a long time going to sleep that night and when she did she slept heavily. She was awakened by a knock on the door. 'Who is it?' she called drowsily.

'It's me—Saul—are you nearly ready? The conference starts at ten, you know?'

'Heavens!' She fell out of bed and dragged on a nylon wrap. She unlocked the door and opened it a crack. 'I overslept,' she muttered stupidly. 'What time is it?'

He pushed open the door further and stepped into the room. In dark trousers and crisp white shirt, his hair tamed to lie nearly flat, he was looking freshly-groomed and alert, ready for an important conference. He was looking, in fact, exactly as she ought to have been looking—and wasn't.

'I'll be quick,' she croaked. 'Just tell me the room to come to and I'll find it.'

He shook his head. 'I'll wait for you,' he said. 'I wouldn't like you to get lost.' He leaned nonchalantly against the window-frame and folded his arms as she began feverishly to pull out drawers and open cupboard doors. 'A pity about last night,' he said easily. 'I wasn't very long getting that idiot Ferguson out of hock. He'd got himself into a fight in a café. He should have known that you have to watch your step with the Mexican girls. Their boyfriends are apt to get very nasty. I hoped you'd still be awake when I got back and we could have shared a nightcap. But there was no answer when I came to your door so I assumed you'd gone to sleep on me again. You make quite a habit of it, don't you?'

'I was tired,' Karen mumbled. She grabbed a yellow-and-white cotton dress off its hanger and made a bee-line for the shower room, trusting she had everything she needed. If that man thought that he was going to stand there and watch her dressing he could think again.

She emerged five minutes later, fully clothed, and sat down at the dressing table to do her face and brush her hair. He was still standing beside the window. 'That must be a record,' he said. 'You're an extremely efficient young woman, Miss Lane.'

'Thank you.' She applied eye shadow and liner deftly and touched her lips with a pale rose lipstick. That was all the make-up she would need this morning. She brushed her dark silky hair quickly and twirled it round, piling it on top of her head.

Saul strolled over and stood behind her. 'A pity you can't leave it loose,' he said. 'I suppose that wouldn't accord with the business woman image you're so keen on projecting?' He bent down and planted a kiss in the nape of her neck, as if it were the most natural and ordinary act, as if they were lovers, or newly-weds. 'For the same reason I've put a tie on this morning— although I expect it'll have to come off before very long. Are you ready?'

'Yes.' The casual caress made her knees shake as she stood up. She tried to think of something ordinary to say and came up with, 'Can I snatch a sandwich on the way? I seem to have slept through breakfast.'

'I've ordered coffee and rolls to be laid on in the conference room,' Saul said as they went out to the lift. 'You won't be the only one who's missed breakfast,' he added drily. He took her arm and hurried her along. 'Come on, we're going to be late.'

The conference room was a large, airy apartment on the first floor, with all the necessary trappings: long polished table with chairs all round, note-pads, pens and pencils, glasses, water-carafes. There was a name-card before each chair. There were perhaps ten or more men already in the room, all of them assembled round the bar at the bottom of the room, where coffee and sandwiches had been laid out, and Saul led Karen straight there and poured coffee for her.

'There you are,' he said. 'Eat your fill,' and turned away to speak to a man on his other side. 'Feeling better this morning, Ferguson?' There was heavy irony in his voice.

Ferguson—that must be the man that Saul had gone to bail out last night. Ferguson was a man of about forty-five, with thinning hair and a pallid complexion. If it hadn't been for you, Karen thought with a twist of her mouth, I probably shouldn't be here this morning with my virginity still intact. Saul had made his intention very clear and at that moment she knew she couldn't have resisted him. She must be more careful for the remainder of the time they were here. Moonlight in Acapulco certainly weakened your defences.

She munched a roll with gusto and surveyed the room and its occupants, some of whom she had seen yesterday, others who were complete strangers. Max

Friend met her glance and immediately came over. 'Good morning, my lovely, you're looking prettier than ever today.'

'Hullo, Max.' She smiled at him, pleased to see someone she knew. He looked attractive this morning; obviously groomed for a business session, his wavy golden hair well combed back, his pale blue shirt and blue cotton trousers freshly laundered. She liked the laughter-lines round his faintly bloodshot blue eyes. If he was a rake he was a nice rake, she thought.

'Had a good dinner last night?' he said, sliding her a wicked glance as he helped himself to coffee. 'I was sad that the Great White Chief plucked you away from me before I had finished telling you my life story. Perhaps I could give you a second instalment later on, when the talking-shop has closed.' He waved his coffee cup towards the long table.

'Perhaps,' said Karen. 'I'm not sure yet what the plans are.' She was here at Saul's request, to further Ben's interests, she mustn't forget that.

Max grimaced towards Saul, who was engaged in conversation with a burly man with white hair. 'Point taken,' he said. 'Ah well, I'll look out for you at the pool. That's the best place to keep reasonably cool at the back end of the afternoon.'

Bill Goodall came trotting up, beaming. 'Good morning, Miss Lane, I have a message for you from my wife. We're making up a little party this evening to see the famous divers at Le Quebrada and we're relying on you to come along. It should be quite exciting. Not to be missed, the tourist books say. May I tell Ann that you'll come?'

'Thank you, I'd like that,' Karen said eagerly. An evening without the risk of another tête-à-tête with Saul was just what she needed, and he could hardly object to her accepting an invitation from the

Goodalls—he had even suggested himself that they should make up a foursome.

'Splendid, splendid, Ann will be delighted.' Bill Goodall moved away to search the table for his name card. The room was filling up rapidly now, and women were decidedly in the minority, Karen noticed. In fact there were only two beside herself. One was a middle-aged woman, very smart in a sleeveless black dress and a swept-back style to her silver-grey hair. The other was young and dark-skinned and was hovering a little uncertainly behind the crush at the buffet table.

Saul turned, looking for Karen. 'Come on,' he said, taking her arm and leading her to a chair round the corner from his at the top of the long table.

Under the buzz of conversation Karen leaned towards Saul and said, 'What do you want me to do? Ben said you needed me to take shorthand notes.'

For a moment he looked bewildered. Then he grinned. 'Oh—that. No, we have little Miss Valero to do that.' He nodded to the girl who had been hovering on the edge of the group and said, 'Pull up a chair here, just behind me, Isabel.' To Karen he added, with a grin. 'You're in an executive capacity now, my girl, not a secretarial one. And anyway——' the dark lashes lowered themselves over his eyes '—that was just a lure to get you to come along.'

Karen caught her breath. He was fooling, of course, she really couldn't believe that she had made such an impression on him at their first meeting. She could feel her heart begin to beat rather hard. Damn the man, why did he have to say that—to muddle her up again just when she was beginning to feel cool and moderately collected.

Saul leaned forward in his large executive armchair at the end of the table and picked up the chairman's gavel. 'Are we all ready?' he said, giving it a couple of light taps on the polished mahogany. He hardly raised his voice, but immediately the buzz of talk and the coughing and rustling of papers ceased and all eyes were turned expectantly on the chairman.

Saul took masterly charge of the proceedings from then on, and Karen could only sit back and admire. He was a born leader, no doubt about that. His personality, his voice, his fluency with words, everything about the man was vital and impressive.

After a short welcoming spiel he paused for a moment and then continued, 'Now, before we start I'd like to make a short announcement. As most of you know, our group has been having some difficulty in obtaining components of various specialised sorts from outside firms and I've been looking at one or two small companies that we might bring into our fold so that we shouldn't have to go outside our own group and run into difficulties over prices and delivery dates and so on. One of them is Clark's Components of Lessington, in the Midlands. Unfortunately Ben Clark, the managing director, can't be with us today but we have his personal assistant, Karen Lane, here. I think some of you have met her already. Karen will sit in on our first session, while we have our general discussion, and report back to Ben. Meanwhile, she will be glad to answer any questions after the meeting, and I hope you will ask her anything that you feel will be useful to you.' He turned and flashed a smile at Karen.

'Miss Karen Lane,' he said formally.

They were all looking at her and there was a murmur of interested voices and one or two desultory hand-claps. She smiled round the table at the faces turned towards her and hoped that her disappointment didn't show. She knew now that she had been half-expecting Saul to announce a firm decision at this meeting, something she could tell Ben straight away. But now it seemed that there was competition. Clark's was the only one of the companies under consideration.

The conference went its predictable way and Karen sat with a fixed expression of interest on her face, but she wasn't following what was being said, she was watching Saul's reactions to what was being said. He had a mind like a rapier, she thought with a twinge of fear. He cut through fuzzy ideas, twisted garbled suggestions into shape, pounced on anything that seemed promising. He seemed to hold this experienced, gimlet-eyed collection of business men in his hand like a deck of cards, playing off one against the other. And, strangely enough, they seemed to like it; there was very little argument. Oh yes, Saul Marston was a winner, he would always get what he wanted, and nobody was going to influence him against his better judgment. Clark's Components would have to take its chance, along with the other 'possibles'. But it was a bad let-down and she thought that at least he might have hinted at the situation and not raise Ben's hopes as he had done.

When the session ended at last the company drifted over to the bar and then settled down in the adjoining lounge in groups of twos and threes to discuss the business of the morning. Saul put an arm casually round Karen's shoulders. 'Well, what did you think?' he said. 'Do you like us? Will you recommend us to Ben?'

She said, 'I thought it was the other way round. That it was up to you to make the decisions. Isn't that what you usually do?'

He grinned. 'Uh-huh, you're getting to know me, Miss Karen Lane—a man with a power complex,

that's me. Now come along and tell me what you want
to drink, and I can see several of our company waiting
to talk to you.

Karen sighed and followed him to the bar. If he had
already decided he wasn't going to tell her.

An hour later she made her way up to her room.
Saul had suggested lunch but she had pleaded a
threatening headache (which was perfectly true) and
he had seemed really concerned and insisted on
coming up with her to give her some tablets that he
recommended.

'Two of these will put you right,' he said, shaking
them from the container and pouring water from one
of the bottles on the side table. 'And by the way, I
shouldn't drink water from the tap. It's probably O.K.
this is one of the better hotels, all the same it's always
a bit of a risk. Now, have a good rest and come down
when you feel like it. We've pushed you rather hard,
haven't we, but you stood up very well to the cross-
examination.

She sat down on the bed and slipped out of her
white sandals. 'You'd better take your dress off too,'
Saul said. 'It's going to get hotter by the minute, even
the air-conditioning can't always cope.

'I will,' Karen murmured. But not with you
standing there watching me, she thought, meeting his
eyes with a little lift of her brows.

He laughed. 'O.K. I get the message, I'll take
myself off. Later on we can make plans for the
evening.'

Karen said, 'The Goodalls have asked me to join
their party to see the Quebrada divers. I think that
includes dinner somewhere, I'm not quite sure.'

He frowned. 'And you promised to go?'

'Yes, of course, it sounded fun,' she said innocently,
but she knew he was annoyed.

Then he shrugged. 'Oh well, so be it. I'll go and invite myself to join the party.'

He walked across the room and pulled the heavy, printed-cotton curtains. 'That will be nice and dim for you,' he said, 'and keep the heat of the sun out of the room.'

He came back and stood looking down at her. His eyes were soft, his mouth tender. He looked oddly understanding and somehow comforting and Karen had a crazy impulse to reach up her arms and pull him down to her.

She drew in an uneven breath. 'Thank you very much, you've been very kind,' she said.

The enigmatic expression that she was beginning to recognise was back on his face. Then he lifted her feet and laid them on the bed and, bending down, kissed her lightly on the forehead. 'See you,' he said and went quickly out of the room.

When the door had closed behind him Karen slipped her dress off and stretched out on top of the smooth bedcover, staring at the ceiling. For a few moments she had thought she saw a new side to Saul Marston. Perhaps he wasn't all the hard, ruthless, success-man who took what he wanted and used his charisma to get it. She sighed and closed her eyes.

The tablets were beginning to make her feel drowsy now. Probably what she had seen in his face had just been a trick of the half-light, she told herself sleepily. She mustn't let herself start imagining that Saul was a caring human being because if she did she might find herself falling in love with him, and that would be madness. What she felt for Saul had nothing to do with what she had always thought of as love. If she let herself be enticed into a purely sexual encounter it would be against everything that she had always believed in.

She had taken part in countless sixth-form arguments about sex, like every other girl, and always she had stuck to her own point of view—that sex just for the sake of sex was somehow belittling. That you must love a man and be committed to him before you made love with him.

She still stood by that position—of course she did. But what she had felt for Saul when he took her in his arms out there in the perfumed dusk of the Acapulco moonlight last night was a throbbing awareness of her own body that she had never felt before. A wanton hunger that shocked and bewildered her.

She mustn't let herself be put in that position again. She must remember Ben, and what she was here for.

But before she finally drifted off to sleep she could feel thick tears gathering behind her closed eyelids and sliding down her cheeks.

CHAPTER SIX

NEARLY two hours later Karen woke up feeling light and happy, for no reason that she could think of. Perhaps it was just Acapulco, it really was a paradise. She opened her window and the warm scented air drifted in, gently caressing her bare skin. Far below, in the dazzling sunlight, the scene was like the pictures from all the travel brochures rolled into one. Blue sky, blue sea, white sand, lush greenery trailing over the rocks, little straw-roofed huts under the palm trees, bronzed bodies in shorts or vivid-coloured bikinis, according to sex. The hotel swimming pool was a splash of turquoise against its marble surrounds. Red canvas loungers fringed its edges temptingly. The faraway sounds of splashes and laughter came up to her as she stood at the window.

She sighed with delight. She couldn't wait to get into that pool. She selected a pink bikini from the pile her mother had bought her as a present on their shopping trip. ('You'll want plenty of bikinis in Acapulco, dear. Jennifer French went there last year and she said you just *live* in bikinis, plus the minimum of covering when you go into the hotel for meals. *She* took lots of pretty little dresses and never put one on.') Karen stood in front of the long mirror, struggling with the fastening of the bikini tip, and giggled at the stir she might have caused if she had walked into the conference meeting this morning in this stage of undress.

The conference! She bit her lip. How unforgivable of her to keep forgetting what she was here for—to look after Ben's interests. She sat on the edge of the bed and picked up the telephone. Surprisingly quickly she got through to the hospital in Mexico City and, concentrating on her Spanish managed finally to speak to the nurse in charge of Ben's ward. '*El Señor Clark?* *Si, si*, he is making satisfactory progress and able to eat a little food today.'

'Oh, I'm so glad. Please tell him that Karen telephoned to enquire and that I will be writing to give him all the news.'

She wrote at length to Ben, with a rather heavily-censored account of everything that had happened since she arrived, concentrating on this morning's meeting, carefully avoiding the fact that Clark's Components seemed to be only one of several companies that Saul was considering to fill the gap in his group. It wouldn't hasten Ben's recovery to know that.

'There are more meetings tomorrow,' she went on, 'but Saul says I won't be needed as they are concerned with policy-making and, I suppose, will be confidential. Everyone has been very friendly and the other directors seem interested in us and have asked me a lot of questions—I think I managed to cope with most of them. Tonight I have promised to go to dinner with a Mr and Mrs Goodall, who are pleasant folk. He's the M.D. of Goodall Faulds, of Birmingham. Tomorrow is the big wind-up dinner of the conference, and then on Saturday we go our separate ways. I shall come straight back to you in Mexico City, of course, and so hope I'll be the bearer of good news for you.

I'm just off for a swim, and so wish you were with me—it's been wretched luck the way things have happened. I've just spoken to the hospital and they say you are feeling much better today—I'll hope to see you looking your old self on Saturday. Thumbs up and fingers crossed! Love from Karen.

P.S. Saul Marchant doesn't really improve on acquaintance. He's very much the Big Tycoon—*and* he knows it. But he's been——'

She stopped, biting the end of her pen. He's been—what? What could she say about Saul? 'He's been trying to get me into his bed and last night it was touch and go'? Put crudely like that it made it all sound so cheap and she felt guilty and disloyal all over again. How could she ever have let things go so far?

She wrote '—he's been reasonably friendly and helped me through the ins and outs of the meeting and introduced me to everyone.'

She sealed the letter and gave it a little pat. 'Ben, I'm sorry,' she said. 'I'm horrid. Forgive me, and get better soon, and let's get back to normal.'

After that she felt a little less guilty, and for good measure wrote a short letter to her parents at home, before she went down for a swim.

Karen floated on her back in the pool. The sun burned through her closed eyelids, turning the world rosy pink. From a great distance, it seemed, she heard voices and splashing and the clink of glasses. She began to paddle with her hands towards the edge of the pool, her body rising and falling gently in the clear, warm water. Heaven must be like this, drifting on a cloud, with no hassle, no worries, no people making demands. Just peace.

'Karen!' A man's voice sounded from the pool-side and her heart missed a beat. Saul! She floundered, went under and came up gasping, swallowing a mouthful of water. A couple of quick strokes took her to the steps and she climbed out—to see Max Friend, in sunglasses and pink shorts over a pale, rather-too-podgy torso, standing there grinning at her.

She tried to push back her disappointment. 'Hullo, Max.'

'My little friend Karen, looking more beautiful than ever.' He took off his sunglasses and his eyes roamed over her shamelessly. 'How come the gorgeous suntan? I didn't know you were a member of the Gilded Set. You make me feel like an undercooked plaice.'

'Gilded Set? Me? I'm a working girl. A few sessions on a sun-bed at the local health club.'

'Ah-ah,' gloated Max. 'Sun-beds, is it? Do they have mixed sunbathing at your health club? I wouldn't mind sharing a sun-bed with you, my lovely.'

'Wouldn't you indeed?' quipped Karen mechanically. This was harmless foolery but very boring and she wished she hadn't been so eager to get out of the pool when she thought she heard Saul calling her.

Max pulled out a couple of the red canvas loungers. 'Relax and dry off, darling, while I go and get us some drinks.'

There was a bar near the pool, under the trees. He came back and handed her a long green drink in a frosted glass. 'Your favourite,' he said. 'I remembered.'

She thanked him and lay back, letting the sun dry her body, sipping the limejuice, her eyes moving round the pool-side.

'Looking for the Big Boss?' Max grinned. 'I saw him some while ago with our Lovely Liz. Talking over old times, no doubt,' he added with a leer.

'What do you mean?' The question was out before she could stop it.

'Don't you know?' Max lay back and put on his sunglasses. 'No, of course, you're a new girl, aren't you? Saul and Liz had a big thing going at our last conference in Geneva six months ago. It seemed to be heading up for the altar and then, all of a sudden, she married Harry Walker.' He chuckled. 'Saul's not exactly the marrying sort, wouldn't you say, and I guess Liz knew which side her fruit-cake was buttered. She probably followed Harry here meaning to have the best of both worlds when Harry wasn't looking. I guess she got a shock when she saw you.'

Karen said coldly, 'I'm really not interested in Liz Walker—and I don't care much for gossip.'

Max grimaced and put up a hand to ward off an imaginary blow. 'Wow! Straight between the eyes! I deserved that—but it was meant as a friendly warning, my poppet. Anyway, he'd be a bloody fool to look twice at Liz Walker when he can look as often as he likes at you. And I bet he's given her her marching orders once again if she's planning a comeback. Saul's not the type to enjoy warmed-up porridge,' he added crudely. 'No, I'd say it's all over between those two. Or——' he paused significantly and gave a low whistle, jerking his head towards the hotel '—or is it?' he added slowly.

Karen followed his glance. Saul and Liz Walker were walking slowly down the path that led from the hotel. They made an eye-catching couple under the canopy of giant tropical leaves—Saul, tall, bronzed, muscles rippling. Liz Walker in a bikini that was little more than two narrow ribbons of a clinging material patterned (appropriately, Karen thought) like snake skin. It didn't seem fanciful to imagine her sliding through the undergrowth, rearing her beautiful head to strike poison from her fangs. She was clinging to Saul's arm, gazing up at him, her russet head pressed against his shoulder as they walked. He was smiling down at her and they looked as if they were glued together. Karen felt a sharp stab of what she recognised as jealousy. Just a gut reaction they called it, didn't they? Just because he had taken her out last night and kissed her. It didn't mean a thing.

She remembered Ben saying that he had heard that Saul had some girl following him round to conferences. Liz, evidently. Probably, in the set they moved in, a little matter like being married to someone else didn't count, she thought with unusual bitchiness. But what did it matter to her what they did? This wasn't her scene and never could be.

Saul detached himself from Liz as they came near and grinned down at Karen, stretched out on her lounger. 'Been swimming, Karen? Wish I could have joined you, but some people have to work. Max, I've been looking for you—Roberts wants to talk to you about that German deal you've been planning together. Could we go up now?'

Max had pulled himself out of his chair and now he groaned. 'O.K. Chief.' He squinted down at Karen. 'Notice how this bloke always appears in time to split us up, darling. Never mind, our time will come.'

He and Saul turned back towards the hotel and Liz sank gracefully into the lounger that Max had vacated. Karen lay back with her eyes closed. The last thing she needed was a cosy chat with Liz Walker. But she opened them again when Liz said, 'How's your man getting on—the one in hospital? Saul told me about the situation.'

This seemed safe ground. 'He's doing very well, thank you. The hospital seems pleased with his progress.'

'That's nice.' Liz felt in her beach bag and put on a pair of huge black-rimmed sun glasses. 'You must have been relieved to hear that.'

'Very,' said Karen.

The sun glasses turned her way. They were the kind that were silvered on the outside and Karen felt as if two searchlights were being focussed on her. 'Yes, it was bad luck, his not being able to attend the conference.' Liz's husky voice seemed to hold some deeper meaning. A little pause, then, slowly 'You must have been desperately disappointed.'

That was a loaded remark if you like. Annoyance began to sizzle inside Karen. '*Ben* was desperately disappointed,' she said coolly.

'Ah!' A slow smile spread over Liz's lovely face. 'I see.' She changed her approach. 'It's very good of Saul to take you under his wing, as your man can't be here.'

Karen glanced around to see if she could get away without being rude, but there was nobody she recognised among the bodies lying round the pool. 'Saul's been very kind,' she said stiffly.

'Kind!' Liz gave a throaty chuckle. 'Saul has many fascinating qualities but I shouldn't put kindness among them. To be kind you need a heart and I doubt if Saul Marston has one.'

Karen pulled herself up in her chair. She felt vulnerable lying back listening to this woman, who seemed more like a snake than ever. Flick—flick—her tongue exuded venom with every word.

'I'm really not interested in Saul Marston's heart, or lack of it,' Karen said. 'I'm here to represent Ben Clark's company and my dealings with Saul are on a purely business basis.'

'Yes?' It sounded curiously like a hiss. 'Well for your own good I'd advise you to keep it that way.'

Karen had had enough of this poisonous woman. She scrambled up and dived back into the pool. The water felt cool and cleansing to her hot body as she swam quickly to the far end. She retrieved her beach coat from where she had left it and ran up the path to the hotel.

'Hullo, Karen, been swimming?' It was Annie Goodall in a tight blue dress and a huge Mexican straw hat. 'You do look stunning, dear, you're so lovely and brown and slim,' Annie sighed. 'I daren't wear a bikini—anyway Bill wouldn't really approve. So glad you're joining our little party tonight, it should be fun. Saul says he's bringing you along, you lucky girl!' She did an expressive double-take.

'Yes, aren't I?' Karen said brightly. She didn't want to discuss Saul.

In her room she stripped off her bikini and stood under the shower. She dabbed herself dry with a soft pink towel and draped it loosely round her shoulders. She was still thinking of that beastly Liz Walker and her innuendoes. It was silly to be upset over her sly hints, but Karen had always responded badly to aggression—it made her feel quite ill. She really must learn to toughen up, she thought, if she wanted to get on in the world of business.

She sat brush-drying her hair in the heat that poured in through the open window, looking down at the scene far below, trying to recapture the light-hearted mood of earlier in the afternoon. The beauty of the place was still the same, but now she felt vaguely depressed. If only Saul would make up his mind about taking over Clark's Components! Suddenly she wanted this conference to be over, wanted things to be normal again, with Ben recovered and the two of them working together happily as they had before—only with the difference that the firm would be on its feet again and Ben wouldn't be worried sick about it.

She sighed and stood up and the pink towel slid from her shoulders on to the floor. At that moment there

was a sharp rap on the door and it swung open to
disclose Saul standing there.

Karen let out a yelp, dropped her styling-brush,
grabbed the towel and wrapped it round herself. It
just about covered her from the waist down. She
tried to hold her arms across the top of her and keep
the towel in place at the same time but it kept
slipping.

'The least you could have done,' she burst out,
crimson-cheeked, 'was to knock and wait before you
barged in like that.'

Saul strode across the room, picked up the brush
and put it on the dressing table. 'Ah, but think what I
should have missed if I had.' The dark laughing eyes
passed over her with undisguised relish. 'I looked for
you down at the pool but you weren't there.'

Karen had felt warm before but now she was
burning all over. She pulled open a drawer with one
hand, holding the pink towel with the other and
rummaged through the contents for some garment to
slip into, but found nothing but a pile of panties and
bras and handkerchiefs. 'Go away,' she muttered. 'Get
out of my room.'

He ignored that and went on leaning against the
window frame. She cast him a quick, flustered glance,
and her inside lurched because he looked so
shatteringly handsome. Down at the pool he had been
wearing a loose shirt over navy shorts but the shirt had
now been discarded. Suddenly she was tinglingly
aware of his magnificent body, only a couple of yards
away from hers. He was so bronzed and fit-looking, a
mat of dark hair on his chest and a small tuft on each
shoulder. She had a crazy impulse to touch the tufts of
hair, to run her fingers through them, to let her cheek
rest against his wide brown chest. He was watching
her with amused eyes. 'Not shy, love? Nobody wears

clothes much in Acapulco. You must have gone topless on holiday before now.'

Once, briefly, she had. But not in a bedroom with the sexiest man she'd ever met looking at her in a way that turned her bones to water.

'I don't take my holidays in such sophisticated spots,' she said.

Heavens, that sounded stilted and up-tight, but he only laughed. 'Really? We must extend your education some time. But right now I propose to take you for a drive. I've finished my business for the day and I've managed to hire a car until Saturday. Come on, darling, put the minimum of clothing over that delectable body and we'll go out and let the wind rush through our hair.'

Imagination is a potent temptress. Karen saw a picture of an open car with Saul at the wheel and herself snuggled against him, the sun warm on her arms, her hair streaming out behind her like the TV adverts. She could almost feel the touch of his skin against her cheek, smell the faintly astringent scent of the cologne he used.

She was lost. All her good resolutions about not being alone with Saul went out of the window. 'I'd like that,' she said, 'only do please go away while I put something on.'

'Must I?' he sighed. 'O.K. I'll be a little gent and wait for you outside the door.'

Ten minutes later Karen was climbing into a sleek olive-green sports car and Saul was easing his long body in behind the wheel. 'Nice little job,' he said, slipping through the gears expertly. 'She's the personal car of the hiring firm's owner. They wanted to palm me off with an ancient Chevvy—then I saw this and used a spot of gentle bribery to get her for a couple of days.'

Karen glanced up under her lashes, her eyes teasing. 'Is that the way you always conduct your business?'

'Oh yes—the only way to succeed. Bribery and corruption with a spot of blackmail thrown in now and then to finalise a big deal.'

Karen giggled. 'You know where you'll finish up, don't you?'

He glanced briefly down at her. 'I know what I want,' he said. 'And I know how to get it.'

There was a tiny pause. Then Karen said, 'Where are we going?' and suddenly found that it didn't matter. It was enough that she was here and that Saul was beside her. This train of thought was dangerous, she knew that, but you couldn't be in Acapulco and resist the holiday mood.

He said, 'Not too far this time. Puerto Marques Bay, for a start. We can have a swim there and get right away from the gang. Then I've got a few other things to show you before we head back to join the party for dinner. I told Annie Goodall we'd meet them at the hotel.'

The afternoon was pure magic. A hazy golden glow hung over everything and the faintest of breezes wafted about lazily, just enough to stir the leaves of the palm trees. The beach at Puerto Marques Bay was smaller, more secluded and less crowded than that at Acapulco and the sea calm as a millpond, with only a smudgy, misty line to show where it merged into the pale blue of the sky.

Karen had covered her bikini with a thin white cotton shift and when Saul said, 'Come on, let's swim,' she threw it off and put her hand in his as they ran down the beach, toes sinking into the hot sand. It was marvellous to be able to run straight into the sea without that preliminary gritting of teeth to meet the shock of cold water that you always had at home, even in the best of summers. Here the water was just about body temperature and closed around you like silk. Karen was a good swimmer and kept pace with Saul as they swam out far enough to get away from the tossing beach-balls and the floating li-los.

She stopped and turned on to her back. 'Heavenly,' she called to Saul, treading water a few yards away. Then he was beside her, floating too, one arm holding her waist and as they lay side by side, gently rising and falling with the sparkling water, Karen thought she had never enjoyed anything so much in her whole life. A purely physical enjoyment that touched something deep and primitive inside her. Later, as they lay on the beach, drying off, she sighed, 'Oh, that was wonderful. I can't think why our remote ancestors ever decided to crawl out of the sea and begin life on the hard unforgiving earth.'

Saul chuckled. 'Life in the sea couldn't have been all that easy. What about the predators?' He turned over on his front and squinted down at her. 'A pretty little morsel like you would have been snapped up in no time.' He made snapping motions with one hand while his head came down to hers and his mouth covered her mouth, his teeth biting gently against her lips, a kiss that went on so long that her limbs melted and she was fighting for breath.

When he lifted his head she gasped, 'All right, all right, you've proved your point. Perhaps a fish's life isn't all bliss.'

He pulled a face at her. '*Wasn't* that bliss then? I must be slipping. Let's try again.' His hand cupped her chin and moved down to her shoulder.

But at his touch she rolled away from him with a little shiver. He was just amusing himself, but she was suddenly acutely aware that even a casual kiss from Saul Marston was enough to set her alight and that was dangerous. 'What are the other things you have to show me?'

The corners of his eyes crinkled. 'You put other things out of my mind,' he said softly. But he got up and pulled her to her feet. 'O.K. let's go then.'

At the back of the beach was a row of shacks selling beer and soft drinks and sea-food. Saul bought prawns and they sat on the warm sand shelling them and piling the shells into a paper bag and drinking a heavenly fruity drink with slices of pineapple floating on the top. Karen had never tasted prawns so fat and delicious and wolfed them greedily, licking her lips.

Saul leaned back against the spiky trunk of a palm tree and watched her. 'You know, you don't look in the least like an up-and-coming young woman business executive at the moment,' he mused. 'I think Acapulco is bringing out the best in you.'

'Or the worst,' mumbled Karen, and then, because when he looked at her like that she felt suddenly stupidly shy, 'I know it doesn't seem like it at the moment but I *am* still here on business, you know. I wish you'd make up your mind about taking on Ben's company. I suppose you wouldn't tell me, would you?'

He said thoughtfully, 'You're keen on this deal coming off, aren't you?'

'You know I am.' She sighed. 'I've told you often enough.'

He grinned. 'Yes, you do go on and on about your loyalty to Ben. Have you considered what might happen if Clark's Components does join my group?'

She frowned. 'I suppose—well—things would go on much the same as usual, except that we'd have more capital to work on, train more staff and so on.'

He shook his head. 'Oh no, it wouldn't be quite as cosy as that. The Lessington works would be used almost entirely for production. All the administration would be done from my London office. Which would make you redundant, my dear. I would probably move you to London. How would you like that?'

She sat up, startled. 'I wouldn't—you couldn't——'

'Oh yes, I could,' he smiled. 'Haven't you noticed I usually get what I want?'

'I'd resign,' she said flatly. 'Anyway, Ben couldn't do without me.'

'Couldn't he? If Ben had to choose between saving his company and keeping you on as his P.A. I think I know which he'd choose. Anyway, this is all hypothetical because I haven't made up my mind about anything yet. I've still got another man coming to see me tomorrow.'

She stared out at the calm, flat expanse of sea with the coloured sails dotted about on it and said, 'I wish I knew what makes men so singled-minded about success. Most of you seem to put it before anything else.'

She glanced sideways at him, regretting the remark almost before it was out. Saul Marston wasn't likely to open up and analyse his deeper motives for her.

But after a moment or two he said, 'I can't speak for the rest of my sex but I know damn well why *I* wanted success.' He turned his head and looked straight at her, then away again. 'I lost both my parents when I was three. I found out years later that it was on a holiday and my mother got into difficulties in the sea. My father tried to save her. They were both drowned. The authorities searched in Mexico and the U.S. but couldn't find any relatives still living—I told you I was a mongrel, didn't I?—and there wasn't much money so they put me in a children's home. It was quite a good home, but if you grow up without parents in what they call a communal environment I think you tend to develop a fighting instinct from an early age, or else you become docile and end up as a yes-man. I never remember feeling particularly docile.' His mouth set grimly. 'I must have been a beastly little boy.'

He drew up his knees and locked his hands round them and stared out to sea and when he went on it was as if he were talking to himself. 'I suppose it all began to change when I was adopted when I was eleven. They were a middle-aged couple—Uncle John and Aunt Brenda, I call them—and they gave me something I didn't remember having before—a real home. They did everything for me. They hadn't a lot of money but they helped me in every way they could and when I left university Uncle John used an endowment policy to buy me a share in a small business making domestic machines—toasters and hand-whisks and hair-dryers.' He grinned reminisc-ently. 'I began in a small way sure enough, but I had developed this driving need to get to the top—perhaps in a way to repay them for what they had given me. In the years that followed it was simply hard work and possibly a knack for buying and selling at the right time.' He shrugged. 'Is that what you wanted to know?'

Karen said, 'And your aunt and uncle? They must be proud of you.'

'Sure enough they are. The funny thing is that they don't really want to take anything from me now that I could give them anything they ask for. I tried to persuade them to let me buy them a new house but no, they simply want to stay put where they've always lived, in a little bungalow in Cheltenham.' He chuckled. 'They did let me pay for a holiday cruise for them last year, though. They enjoyed that.'

Karen said, 'They sound like marvellous people.'

'They are,' he said quietly. He was silent for a time,

smiling to himself, looking out over the sea. Then he stood up and held out his hands to her. 'Look, There's still the rest of the guided tour. I want to show you something quite different now, to prove that you have to take the rough with the smooth in Acapulco. Let's go.'

She put her hands in his and as soon as she felt his touch she knew that she would go with Saul wherever he took her.

After that the day was pure enchantment. 'I want you to see Revolcadero Beach,' Saul said. 'We could take the car on—there's a sort of dirt-track road across the peninsula, but there's a better way of getting there. You can hire a boat and a boatman to take you through a jungle river to get to Revolcadero. I've been that way once and I've always wanted to go again.'

After the glitter and sparkle of the beach the river was eerie and mysterious as the shabby little boat thrust its way through the densely overhanging jungle foliage. Sometimes the branches, with their huge shiny leaves, hung so low that you couldn't see six feet in front of you. And everywhere there was a sense of living things. It was as if the undergrowth was seething and moving with life, seen and unseen. Vividly coloured parrots squawked in the branches, monkeys chattered and bounced about overhead.

Suddenly Karen gave a little gasp and moved closer to Saul. 'What's that?' she squeaked.

A scaly, greenish, creature about a foot long lay on the bank, half hidden by leaves. A dewlap hung under its grinning jaws and a ragged serrated crest ran down its back. Deep-set eyes seemed to be peering malevolently at them.

'We're in luck—it's an iguana.' Saul rapped out a command to the boatman to stop, but it was too late.

The creature had turned and with a tweak of its long tail had disappeared into the undergrowth.

Karen lay back in Saul's arms. 'Phew! I wasn't expecting that. I thought we'd met a dinosaur. Are they dangerous? It looked as if it would like to take a nip at us.'

He laughed. 'Not a bit of it—they're scared stiff of human beings.'

'Well, that's a relief.' She made to move away, but Saul held her fast, his cheek pressed against the top of her head and her inside began its now familiar churning.

'There aren't any crocodiles, are there?' she giggled nervously.

His arms tightened around her as the boatman guided them expertly to the end of the short journey. 'If there were I'd slay them for your protection, my lady,' he laughed.

They climbed out on to a rickety wooden landing stage. 'Oh, but that was simply wonderful,' Karen sighed. 'Thank you for showing it to me.'

'There's more to see yet,' he said. 'Half a mo' while I bribe the boatman to wait. You have to bribe everyone in this place—it's completely geared to tourism,' he grumbled.

Notes changed hands and the boatman pulled his hat over his eyes and settled down happily while Saul took Karen's hand and led her to the beach.

Nothing could have made a more striking contrast to the lazy sun-baked protected beach they had just left. Here there were fewer people, and quite a stiff breeze blew from the sea. Great breakers thundered down on to a bone-white stretch of sand, flinging up spumes of spray into the air. Saul and Karen walked along at the edge of the tide, the breeze in their faces, skipping back squealing like children as the waves curled over and threatened to soak them, and it seemed quite natural to twine their arms round each other's waists, in the age-old fashion of sweethearts. Karen threw back her head and laughed with the sheer joy of it all. 'I see what you mean about taking the rough with the smooth,' she shouted above the boom of the waves.

She looked up at Saul, striding along beside her, head thrown back, dark hair ruffled, cheeks damp with spray and her inside twisted painfully. Heavens, she thought, I'm not falling in love with the man, am I? No, I can't be—not after a couple of days.

It was as if he knew what she was thinking for he lowered his head and kissed her as they walked along, a fleeting kiss that brushed her lips tantalisingly and brought the taste of salt to her mouth, and made her inside shake.

And later, as they climbed back into the boat for the return journey she had an odd feeling that she was entering jungle country in more ways than one.

The sun had set and the lights of the hotels were beginning to twinkle out as they got back to Acapulco. They had a drink in the bar and chatted with some others of the group and then Karen escaped up to her room. Saul went into his room next door and a moment later there was a cheerful rat-a-tat on the dividing wall.

She put her head to the wall. 'Hullo.'

His voice came back quite clearly. 'I'll give you an hour to get ready.'

'O.K.,' she called back. She felt oddly excited, like a teenager preparing for her first date, not what Saul had called an up-and-coming young woman executive.

After she'd showered she lay down on the bed to relax but was up again after less than five minutes.

Resting was impossible, she was thoroughly jittery. She could hear Saul moving about in the next room and she had a sudden appalling need to open the door and rush into his arms. She had to pace up and down and breathe deeply in an effort to steady herself. It was a relief when it was time to put on her dress and do her face.

It was the turn of the little ivory satin number tonight. She smoothed the clinging material down over her hips and her nicely flat stomach. Her suntan had deepened in two days, which helped the general effect. The dress wasn't at all outrageous but at home she would have felt conscious of showing quite so much front and back. Here in Acapulco, however, anything went. This dress was positively coy in comparison with some of the womens' outfits she'd seen last night. She tweaked the narrow chiffon ruffle round the low-cut neck and giggled. No bra— shameless, that's what Acapulco did for a girl.

She had three attempts at doing her face before she was satisfied, but at last she looked in her mirror and approved the effect. Not bad, not bad at all. Her skin had a silky brown sheen, her eyes smiled back at her, satisfactorily deep and mysterious, her lips were touched with a pale pink gloss, her dark freshly-washed hair was brushed loosely back over one shoulder. She smiled secretly at herself and admitted that, whatever the outcome, she had dressed to please Saul.

As soon as she saw him she knew that she had succeeded. He tapped at the door at exactly eight o'clock and this time he waited until she called 'Come in.'

'I'm a quick learner,' he grinned. 'See how I took the hint.' His eyes widened as they looked over her.

'My goodness, you knock me for six, you look—exquisite.'

'Thank you.' She smiled at him. 'You look very pretty yourself.' He was wearing fitted black jeans and an ecru embroidered lawn shirt with a frill down the front. His dark hair was brushed and gleaming, his chin newly-shaved but still with a faint shadow that reminded Karen of tough guys in Western movies. He should be wearing leathers with a holster slung round his waist instead of that fashionable shirt.

He came closer. 'Is it permitted to touch? Very carefully?' She felt his hands at her waist, so gently that there seemed a gap between where electric sparks were flashing. He leaned forward and his mouth brushed hers in a butterfly kiss that sent little shivers all through her.

He stepped back with a sigh. 'That will have to do—for the moment,' he said. 'Shall we go—are you ready?'

She picked up her bag and a lazy white shawl. The chiffon ruffles of her dress passed over her shoulders and down her back to meet at waist-level in the centre, leaving a deep triangle of sun-browned skin. As they walked out to the lift she felt the warmth of Saul's hand on her back and her knees went weak. This was building up to an explosion, she knew that. She didn't know how the evening was going to end, and she didn't dare think about it. Perhaps Annie Goodall's company would provide a calming influence. You couldn't imagine plump little Annie letting her hair down.

Saul seemed to latch on to her thoughts. Going down in the lift he said wryly, I'm afraid this "do" tonight may get a bit tiresome. I wish we could have just gone off somewhere together, but Annie Goodall's a nice little soul, I wouldn't want to disappoint her.'

Four of the party were already ensconced round a table in a corner of the restaurant when Saul and Karen arrived. The two men got to their feet and Annie jumped up, holding out her hands to Karen, beaming with pleasure. 'Oh, here you both are—how splendid. I was getting worried that you couldn't make it. Now, you sit next to me Saul and Karen next to Bill, with Raymond on your other side.'

Raymond was a tall gaunt man who had grilled her unmercifully yesterday about the work that went on at Lessington. He was evidently partnering Mrs Bradley, the only woman director at the conference who, with her short-cropped grey hair, severe black silk dress and incisive voice, seemed to be trying too hard to establish herself in a man's world.

Annie was wearing a fluffy pink dress and looked flushed and pretty. She leaned across her husband and whispered, 'Karen, you look absolutely smashing. Doesn't she, Bill?'

'Indeed she does, my dear.' The look that Bill Goodall turned on Karen's cleavage expressed rather more than his words.

The dinner ploughed its way through several courses. Annie had played safe and ordered American food and the steaks were huge and surrounded by mounds of sauté potatoes, carrots and cut green beans. Karen couldn't finish more than half of it. The conversation was heavy going, with Raymond Dobson, apparently unable to leave the subject of business, on one side of her and Bill Goodall, trying rather feeble little pleasantries on the other. She kept meeting Saul's what-did-I-tell-you expression across the table and having to look away in case she started to giggle.

It was a relief when Bill Goodall said, 'I believe the diving exhibition is going to start. Yes, it is. We'd better go and have a look. It's supposed to be quite spectacular.'

Karen found Saul beside her as all the diners in the room rose and moved across the floor, jockeying to get the best position on the balcony. Saul pushed her in front of him and put both his arms round her, holding her against him. She felt the inevitable reaction of her body to the hardness of his and chattered nervously, 'W-where do they dive from?'

Saul pointed. 'From that ledge, up there.'

Karen peered upwards at the two sheer faces of rock with the narrow crevice between them. The moon had risen and in its light the rocks looked black and forbidding. Surely, surely, they couldn't be going to dive down into that abyss of—of nothingness. She felt her stomach heave.

Annie Goodall leaned towards her. 'Isn't it thrilling?' Her voice was awed. 'Those dare-devil boys! I've just heard that they dive a hundred and thirty feet down between those awful rocks and if they misjudge it or get the tide wrong it——' her voice sank dramatically as she added with a kind of relish '—it would be instant death.' She paused for effect and then added, 'But of course they never do make a mistake, do they, Saul?'

'I hope not,' he said drily.

Karen was icy cold. She could make out the ledge high above and see bodies moving on it, three or four of them. One seemed to be carrying a lighted torch. She stared down—down—down—into the inky black-ness of the sickeningly narrow crevice between the rocks and her stomach turned over and over.

It was years since she'd felt this awful clammy terror, not since a holiday in Cornwall with her parents. A little boy had fallen from the edge of a cliff and been dashed to death on the rocks below. The hotel was buzzing with the details of the tragedy, although the child's family had not been actually staying there. For days Karen had to be persuaded and bullied into going out at all. In her imagination she kept seeing every detail, the child playing happily, the treacherous edge of the cliff, the long-drawn-out horror of his fall, the sea foaming over the spiky, cruel rocks far below, and the tears would pour down her cheeks.

Now it was all happening again and she was going to make a fool of herself. It's all *right*, she told herself, her fingernails digging into her palms, they know what they're doing, they won't be hurt. She stared up towards the ledge, making herself look, because if she saw what was happening it wouldn't be so bad, would it?

A gasp went round the crowd on the balcony and Annie Goodall's voice rose squeakily. 'Oh look, he's going to dive with that torch in his hand. Ooh—he's going——'

A tiny, doll-like figure fell from the ledge down into the inky blackness below, arms extended holding the lighted torch. Another, then another ... Karen twisted round and pushed her face against Saul's shirt like a terrified child. 'I—can't—look any more,' she muttered. 'I think I'm going to be sick.' She was icy cold now, shuddering convulsively, her breath coming in gulps.

From somewhere above her head she heard Saul's voice, low and infinitely comforting. 'It's all right, Karen, it's all right baby. I'll get you out of here.'

Somehow—she never knew how—Saul got her out of the restaurant and into the car. She slumped back, weak and shivering, tears rolling down her cheeks. 'Silly——' she hiccuped. 'I'm so sorry—I'll be all right in a minute——'

'Shut up, love,' he said, putting his arms round her and mopping her cheeks with a soft handkerchief. 'Just relax.'

He held her in his arms until the sobbing ceased. She dried her eyes and blew her nose and pushed his handkerchief away in her handbag. Then she smiled up at him tremulously. 'I *did* make a fool of myself, didn't I?'

He shook his head and in the shadowy dimness of the hotel car-park his face seemed to have softened so that she would hardly have recognised him. 'Vertigo,' he said. 'It can hit anyone, even at second-hand. Especially an imaginative type like you, Karen.'

She managed a small laugh. '*Am* I an imaginative type? I didn't think I was.'

'Perhaps you don't know yourself very well. Perhaps you're just a mixed-up kid.' He chuckled softly. 'You need a helping hand to sort yourself out. Let's make our way back and I'll see what I can do to hasten the process.' He tipped up her chin and peered down into her tear-stained face. 'O.K.?' He brushed her mouth with his.

'O.K.,' Karen said. 'I'm fine now.'

Fine. And terrified. And thrilled. And vaguely guilty. A mixed-up kid was right.

But as Saul drove back through the town to their hotel she knew that she had never been so strangely excited in all her life.

CHAPTER SEVEN

'WE'LL have a drink, you need something to pull you together.' Saul made for the downstairs bar as soon as they were inside the hotel.

Karen hung back. 'No, I can't. There might be some of our party in there. I must look a sight.' Her hand went to her tear-stained cheeks.

He stopped and pretended to examine her face in the brightly-lit reception hall. 'No, my lovely, you couldn't look a sight if you tried. Still, I don't particularly want to meet anyone either. So we'll go up to my room, I've got some brandy there, that'll do you good.'

In the lift Karen parrotted to herself, I mustn't. I mustn't go into his room and drink brandy. It's madness. It would only end one way, feeling like I do. I need time to think——

Saul put his key into the lock, threw open the door and stepped aside with a little mocking bow. 'Enter, madame. Come into my parlour, as the spider said to the fly.'

It was so close to what she was thinking—he must have guessed. If she didn't want to appear a naïve little schoolgirl she must go along with his jokey approach.

But when she still hesitated in the doorway, he put a hand on her arm and drew her gently inside the room. 'Come on, girl, you do need a pick-me-up after that fright. I haven't got rape on my mind, you know. If you're worried, I promise faithfully not to try anything on, or make you do anything you don't want to do. Is that good enough?'

'I suppose so,' she muttered uneasily. She went inside the room and he closed the door behind them.

The room was similar to her own only larger. Instead of an easy chair there was a small sofa, instead of a single bed there was a large double one. Karen averted her eyes from that quickly and shrank into one corner of the sofa. Saul brought her a glass. 'Here you are, one small brandy and water.' He sat down in the other corner of the sofa, leaning back, drink in hand, eyeing her.

She sipped the brandy and coughed nervously. 'I'm afraid I've spoilt your evening, I'm so sorry.'

'Don't be,' he said. 'I've seen the Quebrada divers before. And anyway, I much prefer to be here with you. Tell me, have you always been afraid of heights?'

She shook her head slowly. 'I'm not exactly afraid of heights—not for myself. It's difficult to explain. I just can't bear to see anyone else standing on an edge with a sheer drop below. It's so stupid—I feel such a fool——' she laughed shakily at herself '—but I have to go out of the room if there's one of those old comic films on where people stand on high ledges outside windows and look down——' Her throat clenched as the terror struck again, gripping her inside, and she began to shiver convulsively.

'Tell me,' Saul said quietly. 'It's better out than in, as they say.'

She found herself telling him about the little boy in Cornwall. She'd never talked about it to anyone since, and now the words poured out from some deep, wounded place inside her. 'I'd seen him playing—he was staying at the next hotel—he was a chubby little boy with red hair—he used to wear a blazer that was too big for him——' A huge lump came into her throat. 'Oh lord, I'm going to cry again.'

Saul's arms were round her. Her head was against

his chest and it was solid and comforting. She bit her lip hard and gradually the tears receded, gradually the pictures in her mind faded, and there was nothing but the warmth of his body through the thin stuff of his shirt and his breath lifting her hair where his head rested and the smell of healthy man's skin. A slow beat of excitement began to rise inside her, swelling, taking her over, mind and body. She began to breathe very quickly.

'Saul——' she whispered urgently and her hands went up of their own accord and clasped themselves round his neck. 'Please——'

She lifted her face to his and saw a muscle working in his cheek. His eyes were glittering, black as polished jet under those long curving lashes.

'You're sure?' His voice was low and husky.

He was so close and she was aching to feel his mouth on hers. 'Yes,' she gasped. 'Oh yes.'

He stood up, took both her hands and pulled her to her feet, holding her close against him. Then, while their two bodies were moulded together, he lowered his head and kissed her—a long, sensuous kiss that nearly sent her crazy.

'How does this pretty dress fasten?' he muttered. His hands were on the narrow ruffles of the shoulder-straps, pushing them down over her arms so that her breasts were bare. 'Lovely,' he whispered. 'Marvellous,' and she shuddered as his lips closed over first one soft peak and then the other.

Frantically Karen groped behind her waist for the fastening of her dress and finally released it and the slinky satin fell in a heap to the carpet. The froth of white-lace panties followed. She heard Saul's quick intake of breath and for a long moment his eyes moved over her slowly, his face alight with pleasure. Then he lifted her and laid her on the bed. She stretched out sensuously on the smooth cover, waiting. She felt no shyness now, no shame, no regret. She was in love with this man, deep in love and what she was doing was the only possible thing, she wanted to give as well as take.

He flicked off the main switch, so that there was only a glow from the concealed light over the bedside table. In the shadowy dimness she watched him strip off his thin white shirt and toss it over a chair. His trousers followed, then he was beside her on the bed, his mouth on hers, his hands moving everywhere, awakening sensations that rose and sank like the waves of the sea, taking her body with them, drugged with delight. Her hands went round him, tracing the separate parts of his spine, moving round his hips, holding him against her urgently, telling him that her need was as great as his. He must have known that she didn't need lengthy arousal, that she was as hungry for love as he was himself. Their two bodies moved against each other in a kind of desperation, until at last pleasure rose to an unbearable intensity and she heard her own inarticulate cry joining with his groan of pleasure and fulfilment as he called out her name over and over.

At last they lay still, their bodies entwined, the frantic thudding of their hearts gradually quietening, their bodies cooling. Exhaustion was claiming Karen. She felt so relaxed that she was almost boneless, and a lovely lazy, satiated pleasure enveloped her as she felt Saul gently ease her under the bedclothes and then move back to take her into the circle of his arms.

'I love you, Miss Lane,' he said huskily. 'Very much.'

She sighed blissfully. 'And I love you, Mr Marston.' She cuddled up against him and was almost immediately asleep.

She woke to find the sun streaming into the room and Saul, fully dressed, standing beside the bed. He leaned down and kissed her lightly. 'Wake up, sleeping beauty. Time to come down to the cold hard world of business. We have a meeting at ten. There's a cup of coffee for you.' He pointed to the cabinet beside the bed.

Karen struggled up, stupid with sleep. 'Thanks.' She yawned. 'I don't remember ever sleeping so long before.'

'Ten hours,' he said. 'That should finally make up for all the jet-lag.'

She sipped the hot coffee as he went over to the mirror and raked a comb through his hair and her heart squeezed up as she remembered last night and the feeling of that springy hair under her fingers. She doubted if he was remembering though—he looked very brisk this morning—but of course a night like that wouldn't be earth-shaking for him as it had been for her. He must have had lots and lots of women. Better than her, probably, she thought with a terrible pang of misery.

Not turning round he said, 'I think you should come to the meeting this morning, to savour your success when I make my announcement.'

She nearly jumped out of bed, then remembered that she was completely naked and pulled the duvet round her, which was rather silly after last night. 'Announcement?' she squeaked. 'You mean—you've decided on Ben's company?'

'Right first time,' he said, dead-pan.

She flopped back against the pillows. 'Oh, but that's marvellous—absolutely super. Oh goodness, I'm so *glad*.'

He turned then and came over to the bed. There was a twinkle in his eye and his lips twitched at the corners. 'I could hardly do anything else after last night, could I? You already know how I conduct my business affairs—bribery and corruption, I think we said.'

He was laughing aloud now, the black eyes glinting. 'Now, suppose you get up and make yourself charming to receive the congratulations from the boys. Have you got your key—I'll go and get something from your room for you to cover up with. I'm not having you galloping around the corridor starkers for anyone to see.'

He was back a minute or two later with her beach coat. 'There you are—now hurry. A quarter of an hour?'

She slid out of bed and wrapped the beach-coat round her in one movement. 'A quarter of an hour,' she promised gaily. She was bubbling with excitement and delight. She felt like an overfilled glass of champagne. Of course last night had nothing to do with his decision—he wasn't a man to allow his business judgment to be swayed by a little love-making. No, Clark's Components had won through on its own merits, and what a marvellous change that was going to make. She wouldn't wait to tell Ben.

Karen's euphoria lasted all through the meeting. It put a golden haze over the long conference table, even over the down-to-earth businessmen sitting round it, their shirt-sleeves rolled up, their faces already shiny with the heat. Only Saul looked cool and completely in control of himself and everyone else. Sitting on his right at the corner of the table she glanced up now and again as he made his preliminary remarks, and each time she felt like hugging herself with delight.

She didn't look ahead, this one day was enough, when she could see him, touch him if she stretched out a hand. Perhaps this afternoon, when the meeting was over, they would drive out somewhere together as they had done yesterday. And after the big dinner tonight—surely they would make love again.

She dragged her thoughts back. Saul was making his announcement now, turning to her with a smile. 'Karen should congratulate herself. As I think you'll all agree she has coped with her assignment very competently, and she has been extremely helpful to me.'

She kept her eyes fixed on the polished table top, not daring to look up. After that she concentrated hard on what was said, making notes on the pad before her so that she could give a full account to Ben. Her mind was occupied, but the rest of her seemed to be floating a few yards above the table, on a pink cloud of happiness.

At mid-day a buffet lunch was served in the lounge adjoining the conference room. Everyone, it seems, wanted to talk to Karen. 'I feel like a film star,' she giggled as Saul came up beside her.

'I'm glad you're not,' he said. 'I prefer a girl with intelligence.' He took two glasses from the tray of a circulating waiter. 'Champagne all round,' he murmured. 'We have something to celebrate, haven't we?' His dark eyes glinted wickedly into hers, and she felt the heat rise to her cheeks.

Harry Walker appeared beside them. He lifted his glass to Karen. 'Welcome to the club,' he said. 'When do we meet the absent Mr Clark?'

'Oh, he'll want to contact everyone as soon as possible,' Karen said hastily. 'He was so sorry he couldn't be here.'

Harry nodded and looked across her at Saul and as the eyes of the two men met Karen thought she saw a wariness in both of them. 'This little lady has filled the gap admirably,' Harry said. 'She must have been a great help to you, Saul.'

Saul put a proprietory arm round Karen's shoulders. 'Indeed she has. We've got along splendidly together, haven't we, Karen?'

'I bet you have,' Harry said with a meaningful lift of his heavy eyebrows. The look, the words, might have been merely playful, but he didn't look in the least playful. He nodded to them and walked away. He hadn't forgotten what had been between Saul and his wife in the past, that was clear. Perhaps this smooth, sophisticated 'modern' set wasn't quite so smooth after all, Karen thought.

She turned to look at Saul, to see how he was taking Harry's poison-dart, but he seemed quite oblivious. He was urging her through the crush towards the bar. 'Have you had enough to eat? I haven't.'

They ate tacos with chicken, and drank more champagne and Saul said. The meeting's likely to go on for a while yet. Do you want to sit it out—I don't think you need, it's only routine stuff.'

Karen grinned at him hazily. 'After all this champagne, I might doze off.'

He gave her a significant look. 'That was how it all started, wasn't it? That was when I fell in love with you—when you went to sleep on me.'

Karen went very still. The noisy, chattery lounge faded. Had he really said that—'when I fell in love with you'? She stared up into his dark face, her eyes wide, but he looked very much as usual. Perhaps he had been joking—yes, he must have been joking.

He was looking round the lounge, obviously spotting people he wanted to talk to. He said rather absently, 'Will you be able to amuse yourself?'

'Of course,' she said. 'I'll have a siesta then there's always that lovely pool to swim in.'

He nodded. 'Good idea. I was hoping we could get away together this afternoon, perhaps have another sightseeing trip, but I'm afraid I'm going to be busy tying up loose ends with various people. There's always a lot of that to be done at these conferences. However, there's the big dinner tonight at the hotel. I shall make sure we sit together.' He lifted a hand to a man who was passing. 'Peter, have you got a moment?'

Karen made her way out of the lounge and up to her bedroom, rather relieved to be let off the rest of the meeting. It was beautifully cool up here, with the air-conditioning switched on. She lay on her bed and thought blissfully about Saul and remembered every little thing about the last days here with him, turning each tiny incident, each word, over and over like some priceless jewel. 'I love you, love you, love you,' she murmured languously and with the words on her lips she drifted off into a light sleep.

She didn't know how long she lay there in a dream, half awake and half asleep. Then she was fully awake, hearing movements from Saul's room next door. She glanced at her watch. He must have got through his business early—he would look for her at the pool, maybe come here first.

She slid off the bed and pulled on a flimsy wrapper. A slow heat began to rise through her body, a longing, yearning urgency. If she went to his room—now——?

She opened her door and began to walk towards Saul's room as if she were being pulled by a magnet. Just before she reached the door she heard the soft click of the lift closing and shrank back against the wall. Liz Walker came towards her. She was wrapped in a flimsy sea-green cover-up and her wonderful russet hair hung loose round her smooth creamy shoulders. She stopped at Saul's door; then she saw Karen standing there.

'Hul-*lo*!' A sly smile slid across the crimson mouth and was gone. 'And where are *you* off to so hopefully? We wouldn't both be on the same errand, would we?' She moved her body sensuously and the wrap swung open to disclose her naked body beneath. 'This time, sweetie, I think your services won't be required.'

She took a couple of steps closer until her face was only inches from Karen's. 'Get lost, there's a good girl. Saul is expecting me and we have few enough opportunities, without you butting in. You've served your purpose here, he won't be needing you again.' She stretched out and tweaked aside Karen's cover-up, which was covering nothing. 'Yes, I thought so. Now, off you go and play somewhere else.'

The sea-green wrapper wafted a cloud of perfume as she moved away. Saul's bedroom door opened and closed again behind her and the corridor was empty and still.

Stiffly, moving her legs very slowly like an old, old woman, Karen went back into her room and stood leaning against the closed door. After a time she managed to get to a chair and sat gripping the arms, staring in front of her, seeing nothing.

From the next room she heard the mumble of voices, Saul's deep and measured, Liz's very slow— the seductive quality penetrated even through the dividing wall. I must get out, Karen thought in desperation. I can't stay here and listen to—listen to— whatever's going to happen. She pressed a fist against her mouth like a child.

She stumbled across the room and pulled down the first dress she came to and dragged it over her head. No bikini now, she had to cover her body, after what Liz had seen. Karen could still hear the contempt in her voice. 'Yes, I thought so.' She boiled inside with anger and shame and humiliation.

She pulled on panties and sandals dragged a comb through her hair. From the next room came Saul's laughter and then Liz's husky laugh mingling with his. They would be laughing about her, Liz saying 'I just ran into that little secretary girl hanging around outside your door. You did a good job on her, darling. Harry thinks you're hooked. He doesn't suspect a thing.' That would be enough to make them both laugh. Oh, she hated them, she hated them both, Saul worst of all because he had used her and manipulated her and betrayed her. Nothing could forgive that.

After the laughter there was a long silence and that was worse. Karen put her hands over her ears and inside her head something screamed, 'Get out—get away.'

The corridor was empty, oppressive. She ran to the lift and pressed the button but nothing moved. She flung herself down the stairway, stumbling, hanging on to the rail with shaking hands, pushed her way through the drifting crowd in the lounge, out into the reception hall.

Once out of the hotel she began to run. The sand was hot, burning through the soles of her sandals. At this time in the afternoon the beach was crowded and she had to weave her way through brown, prostrate bodies to get to the sea. At the margin of the waves she stopped running, nearly falling over into the water. She might go on into the sea. She could almost feel the water coming up to her waist, then up to her shoulders, then—oblivion. That was how she felt just now—aching to wash away the bitterness of humiliation.

She began to giggle hysterically. She couldn't even drown herself—not with all these people around. And anyway, Saul Marston wasn't worth dying for. She felt nothing but angry contempt for him.

Fool that she'd been—stupid, credulous fool. Of course—he'd had it all worked out from the beginning. All that talk about coming to Acapulco with him to represent Ben's company—how much had she done? Precious little. Anyway, he'd probably made up his mind about the company even before he asked Ben to come, and bring her with him. She didn't believe now that there were any other companies for him to choose from. Why should he put his accountant in charge at Lessington, pick up Ben's debts, if he didn't intend to take over the company? No, that had just been his devious way of keeping her on tenterhooks because he wanted to use her for his own underhand purposes. All that business about letting the men think she was his girlfriend—*for her protection*—that was just eyewash too. Yes, it all hung together. She was the smokescreen set up round his seedy little affair with Liz—so that Harry shouldn't guess what was still going on between them. Oh, but it was squalid— beastly. She shuddered with distaste.

Max Friend suddenly appeared beside her. 'Where are you off to in such a hurry, my sweet?' He peered into her face. 'Why, what's up, lovie? Something gone wrong? Want to tell Uncle Max?'

She shook her head, biting her lip, not trusting herself to speak and after a moment he tucked her arm in his. 'Let's walk it off then,' he said.

The tide was low, they walked along the edge of the waves. Max said, 'Don't take it to heart, love. Ships that pass in the night and all that. That's how Saul Marston is.'

He knew, he'd seen it coming. And in his own funny way he'd tried to warn her, but she hadn't wanted to be warned. She'd been so pathetically easy to manipulate. Last night she had almost thrown herself at Saul. She'd even imagined she was in love with the man! Moonlight in Acapulco—it had gone to her silly head. She'd been trying to play in his league without knowing the rules. But tomorrow she would get back to Ben—and to sanity.

Tomorrow. But what about the rest of today? Saul Marston still held the future of Ben and Ben's company in his hands and she was still Ben's trusted assistant—here to look after his interests and do the best she could for him. For Ben's sake she had to finish the job she'd come here for, and that certainly didn't include putting Saul Marston down and making an enemy of him. She felt a shiver pass through her as she imagined what his anger would be like. After last night he would be so sure that she would be there for him to amuse himself with, if he felt like it.

A naïve little typist from the provinces—easy game, he must have thought. Too ignorant to understand the accepted ways of the sophisticated set he moved in so he could make use of her if he liked. But he could be wrong, Karen thought, with a sudden flare of anger that dulled self-pity and sparked off pride. It would be pleasant to show the great Saul Marston that he could be mistaken.

She felt hollow inside as she knew what she had to do—the role she had to play. Could she do it? Could she possibly carry it off?

I must, she thought, it's the only way out and it's for Ben's sake.

Max was more sensitive than she could have guessed. He had walked beside her in silence, holding her arm in a companionable way, but now he said, 'Look, we've walked long enough. How about a nice long cool drink? We'll sit and gaze out to sea and I'll finish telling you the story of my life.'

'Thank you, Max,' Karen said. 'The cool drink would be lovely but I'm afraid I shan't have time to hear the story of your life. I want to go and buy a dress to wear at the Group dinner tonight— something really snazzy.' A dress that would renew her confidence. A dress that would establish her firmly on a level with Liz Walker—equally hard-boiled, equally sophisticated. She was going to act her head off—and act her heart out. She smiled at Max. 'Want to come and help me choose?'

'I wouldn't miss it for all the tea in China,' Max Friend assured her. 'Tonight you shall be the Queen of Acapulco.'

The sun had set by the time they got back to the hotel. Karen looked round anxiously and through the open door of the main lounge she saw Saul sitting at a table with three other men, deep in conversation. She hurried to the lift and took the dress-box that Max was carrying.

'Thank you for—for being so nice,' she said lamely.

He grinned back at her. 'Friend by name and friend by nature. I'll be rooting for you tonight. You'll knock 'em all sideways in that dress.' He raised both thumbs as the lift took her upwards.

An hour later Karen stood in front of her long mirror and wondered if she had the nerve to go down in this dress. If it hadn't been for Max's encouragement she doubted if she would ever have used nearly half her remaining store of pesos to buy it. It was outrageous—sensational—a dress she would have never in a million years have dared to wear at home. A short, pencil-tight black skirt, topped with a bodice that was hardly a bodice at all, merely a flyaway assortment of enormous taffeta bows in a startling petunia-pink, held up round the neck with a narrow ribbon, and cinched in tightly round the waist with a broad black patent belt. Black lace tights and black sandals with five-inch heels. Petunia lips and finger nails. An eye-make-up called Black Grape. Karen drew in a long breath through pursed lips. She needed a stiff drink to supply a little courage.

Just one drink, though, and she must be very careful how much wine she drank at dinner. She needed to keep her cool this evening. She took one of the miniature bottles from the tiny built-in bar fitment, mixed a gin and orange and tossed it off. Now, she assured herself, she was ready to play Saul's game on his own level.

Right on cue there was a tap on the door and Saul himself appeared. 'How's it going!' he began and then stopped short, black brows shooting up. He looked her over slowly from head to foot and back again. 'What in God's name have you got on?'

Karen spun round, her eyes dancing. 'I felt like celebrating, so I went out and bought a new dress to wear at the dinner this evening. Max came with me.'

'Max?' His lip curled. 'Yes, I can recognise his taste. Why couldn't you have asked me?'

'Oh, I should have done only you said you were going to be busy. Wouldn't you have chosen this?' she asked innocently.

'No,' he said. 'It's too far out for you. Not your style, Karen.'

She dabbed perfume behind her ears and on her wrists. 'Oh, don't be stuffy, what's wrong with it? It's a fun dress—everything's fun in Acapulco. You don't take anything seriously that happens here.' She looked at him under her eyelashes. 'Hadn't you noticed?' She picked up her bag and ran past him to the door. 'Come along, let's go down and join the party.'

Everyone was gathering in the bar for drinks and Karen managed to get separated from Saul. She smiled brilliantly at Max as he made a bee-line for her. 'How do I look?' she whispered conspiratorially.

'Fabulous. All the men are pop-eyed.' He led her to a lounge sofa and sank down beside her. 'Not only the men. Don't look now but Liz Walker is turning bright green. You've certainly put one over on Her Highness.'

Liz was sinous and sultry in clinging burnt-orange velvet, slit to the thighs and backless, with a plunging neck-line and enormous glittering pendant earrings.

'Everything on show in the window,' chortled Max. 'I prefer your bows—you have to look round corners to see the interesting parts. Oh yes, you're going to be the tops tonight, you'll see. Here they come already.'

Three of the men were approaching, and a couple more joined them, crowding round Karen, plying her with drinks, making rather feeble jokes. Soon she found herself surrounded by the very men who only this morning had acknowledged her presence at the conference table politely but without any particular enthusiasm.

She laughed at their jokes and quipped back, her hazel eyes sparkling wickedly. Most of them, she saw, had already been drinking and one man, a pale, balding individual whom Karen recognised as Ferguson, the man that Saul had bailed out the other night, moved closer to her on the cushioned seat and whispered, 'How about a little dinner when I come up to Lessington, darling?'

His arm went round her waist and at that moment Saul broke through the crowd. 'Come on all of you, dinner's on.' He gave Ferguson a dark look and took Karen's hand to pull her up. 'Where did you get to?' he said in a low, annoyed voice as they made their way to the big table set for the whole party in the restaurant. 'I've been looking for you.'

She said, 'I've been mingling—I feel I'm quite one

of the gang now, they've all been so sweet to me—welcoming me and making me feel at home.'

'I bet they have,' he said, with a rather sour glance at the huge cyclamen bow that was brushing his shoulder. 'They're O.K. but I'd prefer it if you stuck by me for the rest of the evening.'

She flashed him a provocative smile. 'I won't promise.'

Karen sat next to Saul, with Bill Goodall on her other side, and Annie beyond him. Liz Walker, Karen was relieved to see, was holding court at the far end of the table. Annie leaned across and said, 'Are you feeling quite better now, Karen dear? Such a shame you had to leave last night. Saul told us this morning that you weren't feeling too good. Something you ate, perhaps?'

'Perhaps,' Karen agreed and felt her inside squirm momentarily at the memory of last night and all that had happened. 'But I'm fine now, thanks. Quite ready to wolf all this lovely food.'

Bill Goodall looked doubtfully at the menu card. 'It all seems to be foreign stuff—what's this turkey with guacamole and prawn enchil—something or other. I'd rather have a steak and chips.'

His wife gave him a reproachful look. 'Don't be insular, dearest. Mexican chefs are supposed to be the best in the world. And look at those marvellous bowls of fruit. I simply adore papayas and mangoes, don't you, Karen?'

As well as the colourful splashes of fruit the long table was decorated with great Aztec pottery bowls spilling out tropical flowers, scarlet and white and blue. 'I think that's intended to be a compliment to the Union Jack,' Saul murmured, leaning towards Karen, putting a hand on her knee under the table. She felt nothing but angry revulsion as she had a vivid, treacherous picture of those hands caressing Liz Walker only a few hours ago. But the act must be kept up. She covered his hand with hers, drawing it higher still, smiling up at him with a little sexy smile before she pushed his hand away with a playful tap.

It must have been a marvellous dinner—Karen just wished she could have appreciated it—even tasted it. She was so tense that she couldn't do either. Turkey—chicken—exotic sauces—the little pancakes called tacos stuffed with all manner of rich goodies—delicious iced desserts decorated with dices of melon and strawberries. Normally she would have relished a meal like this but tonight she only picked at the food on her plate and took tiny sips of wine to make it last longer.

There was an air of *bonhomie* around the table, of a conference successfully concluded, and the men were in high good humour, Karen joined in everything, flirting with her eyes with all the men near her at the table, laughing delightedly as their jokes got more and more risqué. Once or twice she caught Saul glancing at her in a puzzled way and she flashed him a brilliant smile that said, 'Isn't this all *fun*?' She had to go on acting, she had to establish her new personality as a modern girl who would spend a night in a man's bed without a second thought, and no strings afterwards. She had to be armed against him when the crunch came.

The meal seemed endless, the party became more and more hilarious, the dancing and singing of the small group that provided the floor-show added to the general noise and colour. Then the lights were dimmed and soon the small floor-space was thronged with couples, jiving or clinging as the mood took them. Karen's head was beginning to ache and she got up to make her way to the ladies' powder room, but she felt an arm grab her and pull her on to the dance floor.

'C'mon sweetness, dance with me,' a slurred voice breathed alcoholically in her ear. The Ferguson man, and very, very drunk. Karen looked round in the dimness for Saul and saw that he had moved up to the other end of the table and was sitting with Harry and Liz and the woman director.

She tried to wriggle away, but Ferguson held her tightly round the waist. 'Pretty girl,' he mouthed. 'Too pretty for an old bus'ness con-conf'rence. Had me eye on you right from th'start.' He was panting now and his free hand was roaming all over her, damp and hot on her bare back, finding its way beneath the taffeta bows. His mouth opened and clamped down on her neck, wet and slobbering.

Utterly repelled, Karen made a desperate movement to get away from him but his hands were everywhere, like horrible fishy tentacles. 'Let me go,' she hissed. 'Let me *go!*'

'Not on y'life, baby. You stick by me—have a good time together, what?'

A man's arm came between them. Bill Goodall's voice said firmly, 'Just lay off, Ferguson, will you?'

Until now Bill had seemed to Karen a mild little man, but at this moment he was very much the managing director, speaking with the voice of authority. Ferguson's hands went slack on Karen's body and then dropped to his side. 'None of your business, mate,' he hiccuped. But Bill had Ferguson firmly by the arm and was propelling him none too gently away.

Karen pushed through the crowd of dancers and reached the ladies' powder room. Here she sank on to a stool, her cheeks flushed, her eyes bright with anger and disgust.

A moment later Annie Goodall rushed in bubbling with indignation. 'That awful man—he shouldn't have been allowed at a conference like this. He's not even a director, only a rep. of some sort. Has he upset you, my dear? Bill's dealing with him.'

Karen pushed back her hair with fingers that shook. 'It was good of Bill to rescue me. I'm quite all right now—only annoyed.' She laughed. 'Ferguson *is* rather a pain, isn't he?'

Annie put a kind hand on her shoulder. 'You stay with us, dear, for the rest of the evening—we'll look after you.'

Karen thanked her. 'But I think maybe I've had enough. Anyway I was intending to disappear when that man grabbed me. My head's aching a bit—I think maybe I haven't quite got over last night yet. I'll go up to my room and have a good sleep. Will you make my apologies if anyone asks?'

Annie's plump face immediately became concerned. 'You poor love, yes, of course I will. Shall I come up with you, is there anything I can do?'

Karen shook her head and thanked her. Annie was a dear, kind soul but Karen had to be alone.

It was very hot in the restaurant and she made her way round the edge of the room, past the service trollies, as far away from the dance-floor as possible. The noise of the exuberant Mexican band beat through her head until it felt like bursting. She had to pass near the dance-floor momentarily, to get to the exit door and at that moment Saul danced slowly past with Liz Walker in his arms, coiled round him like a serpent.

Karen stumbled out into the cooler air of the wide hall. She was sure that Saul hadn't seen her, but it didn't really matter. He had Liz for the moment because Harry had been lolling back in his chair with too much tequila inside him, for the last half hour, and wouldn't notice what his wife was up to. Saul wouldn't be able to have Liz for the night though, they wouldn't be able to engineer that. And that was when Karen had to be ready to finish off her act.

It was cool in her room, a relief to strip off the taffeta bows and get into a light cotton dress. She wouldn't risk a flimsy robe just now. If Saul came that might look as if she were expecting a re-run of last night. She washed off her make-up and settled down in the easy chair, picking up a magazine. Not until she finally heard Saul come up and go into his own room and close the door would she risk getting into bed. She guessed that wouldn't be for some time. Harry Walker wasn't going to sober up just yet, and Saul and Liz would doubtless make the most of their opportunity.

In the event it couldn't have been more than ten minutes or so before she heard him moving in the next room. She sat gripping the arms of the chair, waiting for the knock on her door; he must surely come, even if only to know why she had left the restaurant in such a hurry.

She had just time to get up and fish out her travelling case and open a few drawers when there was a knock and Saul was inside the room. Karen drew in a ragged breath before she fixed a bright smile on her mouth. She hadn't expected that the mere sight of him would flood her with such wild sensual longing.

'Annie said you weren't feeling well,' he said. 'What's wrong?' She thought she heard a faintly wary note in his voice.

So Annie had been tactful about not mentioning the Ferguson episode and Karen was grateful. She had to act now for all she was worth and if he had known about that it might have complicated matters. 'Nothing's wrong, actually. I thought I'd come up and get packed, I want to make a very early start in the morning.'

He came a little further into the room. 'There isn't any very great hurry, is there? I thought we might go as far as Mexico City together, but I can't very well rush away myself. We could get the afternoon shuttle.'

She shook her head, smiling, shrugging. 'Sorry.'

There was a silence while she transferred a small pile of garments to her case. He came up behind her and put his arms round her waist. 'Karen?' he said softly.

Oh no you don't, she thought. She wriggled away and went to the closet, unhooked her dresses from the rail in one heap and dropped them on the bed. 'I really do have to pack,' she said pointedly, still smiling.

She saw his face change, he'd got the message now. His mouth compressed. 'What's wrong, Karen?'

'Wrong?' she said brightly. 'Nothing's wrong, everything's marvellously right. I've got everything I hoped for when I came here.'

His face was closing up now; he looked like the Saul Marston she had first seen in Clark's office in Lessington—the man she had disliked on sight.

'Because I've come down in favour of Ben Clark's company?'

'Yes. Exactly that.'

There was a long silence. Karen began to fold up her dresses, hoping that he wouldn't see how much her hands were shaking. At last he said in an odd, stiff voice, 'And what about us? What about last night?'

She laughed, her eyes dancing. 'Oh, last night was super. You're a marvellous lover, as I'm sure you know. And,' she added slowly, 'there's nothing I wouldn't do for Ben, anyway.'

That had been a mistake, that last bit. She knew

before it was out. She saw his face harden and a tremor of fear passed through her.

'You mean—you really thought if you slept with me it would soften me up? Turn the choice in favour of Clark's company?'

'We-ell, something like that,' she murmured. 'You said it yourself—what was it, bribery and corruption with a spot of blackmail thrown in.'

He exploded then. 'You little bitch—you knew bloody well I was joking when I said that.' He was white with anger now. He put his hands on her shoulders, shaking her.

Karen moved out of his grasp, with a little chiding smile. 'I never know exactly what you mean—you enjoy being enigmatic, it's part of your image. Anyway, I thought it might just tip the scales in our favour. And it *was* fun, wasn't it?'

'Fun!' He ground out the word through his teeth bitterly and she could almost imagine he cared. 'Is that how it seemed to you? You're a bloody good actress then.'

She touched his hand. 'Don't be cross, Saul, and let's be friends. We may meet again—on business, of course—and we don't want to be on bad terms. Although,' she added for a good measure, 'I don't suppose I'll be working at Clark's much longer. Being Ben's wife is going to be a full-time job.'

He breathed in hard through his nose, his mouth grim. 'So—you've made up your mind, have you, now that Clark isn't going into the bankruptcy court after all? And what will dear Ben think about your little caper last night—all undertaken in his interest—*of course.*'

She pouted prettily. 'Oh Saul, you really are being horrid. You wouldn't tell him, would you?'

He looked at her so contemptuously that her inside

turned to ice. 'No, he said, 'I wouldn't tell him.' He spun round and strode towards the door. 'O.K. if that's how you want it, Karen, so be it. You can tell Clark I'll be in touch with him as soon as I get back from Japan, in about a fortnight.'

He put one hand on the door-knob. 'I suppose you'll be travelling back with him to look after his comfort on the journey?'

'Oh yes, of course,' she said.

'Yes,' he said in a clipped tone. 'Of course. Nanny in action once more. How nice for you both. Good night, Karen.' He closed the door behind him with a restrained slam.

She finished packing, moving like a robot, leaving just her toilet things to put in in the morning. Little knots of tension began to ache, in her shoulders, in her jaw, in her head. It had all gone as she had planned, she hadn't given herself away, she had salvaged her self-respect—in a negative kind of way. Saul had only been marginally annoyed, his pride had suffered a tiny dent, but he would have forgotten all about it by tomorrow.

She wished she could believe that she would too. She just hoped she wouldn't see him again for a long, long time.

CHAPTER EIGHT

KAREN had hoped to leave without seeing Saul again but it was not to be. When she got down to the reception desk next morning, all packed and ready to leave, he was there, leaning against the counter, chatting to the pretty girl on the other side of it.

He saw Karen and came up beside her. 'Good morning.' He turned a pleasant, non-committal smile on her. 'Sleep well?'

She had hardly slept at all. 'Very well, thank you.'

'Good. I thought you might be making an early start and I wanted to make sure there weren't any snags for you to cope with.'

'Thank you,' she said rather blankly. She hadn't expected this, but evidently Saul had decided on his approach to the situation between them. Friendly, businesslike. Well, that was how she had planned it too.

'How are you fixed for currency?' he asked. 'Your bill here will be paid, of course, and your shuttle back to Mexico City. You already have your return flight to the U.K. booked for—when?'

'Er—Sunday,' she said faintly. He might have been briefing a subordinate going on a business trip. She supposed that was how he saw her now.

'But what about Ben—have you considered him? I don't suppose he'll be ready to travel tomorrow.'

'I—I don't know. No, he probably won't.' She was really handling this very badly. An efficient personal assistant should be taking all this in her stride. But

163

she'd had a wretched sleepless night and Saul's presence was playing havoc with her self-possession. She made an effort to concentrate on what she was saying. 'I'll have to see how Ben is when I reach the hospital, and then perhaps arrange to postpone our flight.'

'Yes—well—I'm sure you're quite capable of handling all that.' He sounded rather bored now. 'When you're ready I'll drive you to the airport and book your flight. I'm not sure what time the morning shuttle leaves, you may have to wait.'

'There's no need to bother you,' she said quickly. 'I can get a cab.'

'No bother. Is this all your baggage?' He picked up her travelling case. 'Come along then.' He led the way out to the car.

She sat stiffly beside him in the hired sports car. Not much longer now and then it would be over. If only she could just keep a grip on herself for as long as it took! She said brightly, 'So you're off to Japan?'

He nodded, his eyes on the road ahead. 'Tomorrow morning, I'm flying direct. You're in the team now so I can tell you—I'm planning a tie-up with a Japanese company. If it comes off it'll be the biggest thing I've handled. You'll be hearing all about it in due course.'

'It sounds exciting,' Karen said primly. 'I wish you success.' She looked at his hands on the wheel, the brown sensitive fingers, the gold watch-bracelet, the fine dark hair on his bare forearms. Oh God, why couldn't he have just put her in a taxi? Why did she have to endure this desolation?

He went on talking about his plans, he sounded enthusiastic and excited. 'Your Ben and his designs may fit in very well if this new venture comes off,' he said. 'I've got all sorts of ideas for Clark's Components.'

'Really? That's splendid.' She was near to breaking point—in another minute she would begin to howl and make an utter fool of herself.

They arrived just in time to save her from that last indignity. The very act of moving, walking, getting away from the intimate closeness of the car gave her a respite.

Saul handled the formalities rapidly. 'You're going to have a bit of a wait, I'm afraid. Sorry I can't stop and buy you a coffee. Think you can manage now?'

'Yes, thank you, and thank you very much for your help.' Go, please go quickly, she was screaming inside.

He smiled down at her cheerfully. 'My regards to Ben. I hope you'll find him much improved. Tell him I'll be in touch as soon as I get back, he should have got into harness again by then. There'll be a good deal of legal stuff to get through.'

'I'll tell him,' she said. 'Have a good trip.'

'Thanks,' he said. 'Goodbye, Karen, I'll be seeing you.' He bent his head and kissed her cheek lightly—the casual kiss of a friendly colleague. 'Cheerio.'

She stood like a statue and watched him thread his way through the crowd in the airport concourse, his dark head way above everyone else's. Finally he was gone, without looking back.

Only when a fat lady carrying a plastic duty-free bag barged into her and apologised, did Karen move. Then, with feet like lead, she dragged herself to the nearest coffee bar and crept into a corner, handkerchief held in her face, shoulders shaking.

She should have been relieved, it had all gone just as she had planned. Saul had been taken in by her act and had crossed her name off his little black book of available females. Ben's company had been saved, his future seemed assured. But it was a future in which she wouldn't have any part.

She wrapped her cold hands round her coffee mug and stared blindly out over the moving crowds on the concourse to the place where Saul's dark head had disappeared. And she knew that, in spite of everything he had proved to be, and the way he had treated her, she had nothing to give to any other man until this sharp urgent longing for him had gone. Just now she couldn't imagine that happening.

By the time Karen arrived in Mexico City, booked a room for the night and deposited her luggage, and finally reached the hospital and tracked down the ward to which Ben had been moved, it was early afternoon. She stood just inside the doorway of the large, airy room, her eyes searching for him among the occupants of the dozen or so beds. There were visitors at most of the beds, chairs pulled up, lockers piled high with fruit and books and parcels. A bank of flowers ran down the centre of the ward on a long table, their perfume filled the air. A buzz of conversation rose and fell.

Ah, there he was, in the bed right at the very end. Karen fixed a happy smile on her face and hurried forward. He had seen her and raised a hand in greeting, and a huge grin lit up his nice face, which was so much thinner than when she last saw it.

She leaned over the bed and he enveloped her in a surprisingly strong hug as she kissed him. 'Marvellous—I've been expecting you, Karen,' he said. 'Pull up a chair and make yourself at home.'

Warmth flooded through her, it was so lovely to see Ben again, and looking his old self. She hadn't realised until this moment quite how much he meant to her. She looked round for a chair and saw what she had missed before, in the flurry of greeting. On the far side of the bed, looking very much at home herself, sat Jean McBride.

Karen gasped. 'Jean—I didn't see you before. What a surprise—when did you get here?'

'Hullo, Karen.' Jean didn't quite smile, in fact she looked decidedly ill at ease. 'Och, I came a few days ago.'

The two girls looked across the bed at each other and there was an awkward silence. Then Jean got to her feet and said, 'I'll be getting along, Ben, for the time being, now you've got Karen to talk to.' She picked up a bulky carrier bag. 'I'll see to your laundry and try to get that book you wanted.' She laid a hand on his shoulder briefly. 'See you soon,' and with a nod towards Karen she walked quickly away down the ward.

Karen sank into a chair. 'Well! How amazing to find Jean here.' She was utterly at a loss for words.

Ben said, 'I was amazed myself when she walked in. She's been rather splendid really, looking after all my little needs, seeing to my laundry, bringing me books to read, fixing up with the bank and insurance at home about paying the bill here. Yes, she's been very helpful. But let me look at you, Karen—you're looking marvellous. All that Acapulco sunshine?'

'I wish you could have been there,' she said, 'you'd have loved it. I've got such a lot to tell you, I don't know where to begin. But first of all——' she leaned towards him '—how are you, Ben? How's it been?'

'Not too bad,' he said. 'The first couple of days were a bit ropey but since then there's been a steady improvement. The doc is quite pleased with me, says

I'll be fit to travel in a week, all being well.'

'That's splendid,' Karen said warmly. 'I've thought about you such a lot. And I've got good news for you, Ben. About Saul Marston and the company.'

He nodded, his eyes shining. 'I know, my dear. Saul telephoned yesterday and I was able to speak to him myself. Good news indeed—the best. The nurses here were amazed by the way my temperature suddenly came down. You've been doing splendid work at the conference, Saul said. He seemed most impressed by you. You got along O.K. with him?'

'Oh yes,' she said, not quite meeting Ben's eyes. 'He's a keen businessman and he's got lots of new ideas. I think Clark's will come quite well out of the deal. Would you like to hear all about the conference?'

It wasn't easy, picking out the bits that would interest Ben, carefully avoiding anything that seemed to link her with Saul, but somehow she managed it. 'I think that's the lot,' she said finally. 'They seem a very good group of companies, I'm sure you'll like the managers and directors and work well with them. I found them very helpful.'

There was a silence. He was looking at her oddly. 'Karen——' he began.

Oh no, she thought, I can't let him say it. She hurried on, pretending not to hear, 'We'll have to make arrangements about travelling, Ben. We've got our flights booked for tomorrow—had you remembered? We'd better do something about that.'

He sighed and a cloud seemed to pass over his face. Then he grinned, his old wry grin. 'Jean's seen to that,' he said. 'Most efficient, she's been. She's cancelled my flight and arranged to re-book as soon as I can travel.'

'But what about mine?'

'She left that as it is,' he said, watching her face. 'She thought you would probably need to get back to the office to see this Ward man who's functioning there. It seems that he could do with some help.' He paused. 'She—Jean, that is—has offered to stay on and help the poor invalid with the travelling snags.' He made a wry grimace.

'Oh,' said Karen rather blankly. 'What about her grandmother? I thought Jean had to look after her.'

'She died just recently, it seems,' Ben said. 'Jean's on her own now.'

'I see,' Karen said. She did see. Jean was on her own at last, free to put in a bid for Ben and that was just what she was doing.

'Jean seems to have it all fixed up,' she said.

'Not quite.' Ben put out a hand and covered hers. 'You could stay, Karen, and send her back on your ticket.'

They both knew what he was saying, it didn't need the words. There was a silence and Karen looked down at her hands. Then, very slowly, she said, 'I think—perhaps—it would be better if Jean stayed.'

He went very pale. It was awful to have to hurt him before he was really better, but it would be even worse to act a lie. She said gently, 'I'm so sorry, Ben——'

After a time he said jerkily, 'I see. Well, it serves me right. I think I knew the danger when I asked you to go to Acapulco with Saul Marston, but all I could think about was the company.' His mouth twisted. 'The company came first, before everything. I'm being brutally honest with myself.'

That was what Saul had said. If Ben had to choose between you and his company I know which one he'd choose.

Ben went on slowly, 'Afterwards, when I let myself

think about it, I knew that Saul Marston would look at you and want you—what man wouldn't? It *is* Saul, isn't it?'

'How did you guess?' she said wearily. 'Is it so obvious?'

'Your letter,' he said simply. 'And—the way you look. And the way you *don't* talk about him. It's obvious to me.'

There was a short silence. Around them visitors were preparing to leave, there was kissing and messages and get-well-soon.

'Is it——' said Ben. 'Are you——?'

'No,' Karen said quickly. 'It isn't and we're not. In fact, what there was is finished but—oh well, never mind, let's not talk about it.'

She drew herself up in her chair and sat very straight and businesslike. 'O.K. Ben, I'll take the flight tomorrow as planned, and go into the office on Monday and see what I can do to help Mr Ward until you get back. Then——' she said slowly '—I think it would be better if I bowed out altogether. Saul made quite a point that I shouldn't be needed in Lessington, under the new organisation plan. He suggested I move to the London office but I certainly shan't do that. I'll probably stay at home and lend a hand in the practice. My father can always do with help.'

Ben's eyes were searching her face pleadingly. 'But we won't lose touch, Karen? You'll come along to the works and see how we're getting along sometimes?'

'Of course I will,' Karen said warmly. 'I shall love to come and see you all.'

He nodded. 'That won't be so bad then.'

She blew her nose hard. She was near to tears. She picked up her brief-case and laid it on the bed. 'Everything's in here,' she said. 'The notes I made at the meetings and the names and addresses of all the firms in the group and their directors, and their various interests, and little bits I picked up while talking to some of them. Copies of reports—there'll be enough to keep you interested for hours.'

She stood up. 'I'll go now. Don't work too hard, Ben, and get tired.' All right, Saul Marston, I'm being the nanny, so what? It's for the last time.

She leaned over and kissed his cheek. 'Get quite better, won't you, and I'll see you when I get back.'

'Karen——'

'Yes?' She waited.

Ben smiled his quiet smile. 'Just—Karen. And thank you.'

She smiled back and walked blindly down the ward. At the door she half turned and lifted a hand and then hurried away down the stairs and out of the hospital.

In the days that followed, the English weather provided a perfect setting for Karen's state of mind; everything was frozen and lifeless. A January freeze-up had set in, they told her, just after she left for her wonderful trip into tropical sunshine. Her mother, brisk and busy as ever, looked at her consideringly and said, 'You've browned-up nicely, but you've lost weight, haven't you? Didn't the food suit you?' Her father was more penetrating. 'It wasn't all you hoped, was it, love? Something went wrong?'

She put a bright smile on her face and fielded all their questions with the explanation of too much air-travel, and being worried about Ben's unfortunate illness. She'd be fine and back to normal in a few days, she assured them, and they were both much too busy to probe into the results of the trip. She'd have to tell them some time that she was leaving Clark's. Just now she hadn't the heart.

She hadn't a heart at all, she thought sometimes as she dragged herself backwards and forwards to the office, only a heavy lump inside where her heart ought to be. Saul had plucked her heart out of her and thrown it away—what would he want with hearts anyway?

The office was in a depressing state of being run down. Little Lucy had left already to go on a hairdresser's training course. James Ward, an efficient young man with sleek black hair and horn-rimmed glasses, seemed to Karen to be playing the part of an undertaker. He had brought a personal computer with him and sat in front of it all day doing complicated things with accounts and records. In between times he did his best to chat up Karen, without much success.

'Would you like me to show you how this little beauty functions, Miss Lane?' he suggested hopefully. 'You'll need the know-how if you join us at the London office.'

'I shan't be joining you at the London office,' Karen said.

Young Mr Ward looked slightly crestfallen. 'Not? Oh, I'm sorry. Mr Marston said——'

'I shan't be coming to London,' Karen said again, finally and definitely and after that he gave it up and left her alone.

The work of the factory went on as usual; orders were executed and despatched but no new orders were coming in, and Karen found out from James Ward that all their customers had been advised of the reorganisation of the company. 'We shan't be accepting orders from firms outside the group,' he said. 'Mr Marston said to run down local commitments.'

'I see,' Karen said bleakly. She supposed it was all according to plan and would work out well, but she couldn't help feeling that she was attending a very long-drawn-out funeral, in which she herself was the principal participant.

A week after Karen had returned Jean appeared at the office. A brand-new Jean in a smart dove-grey suit, her sandy hair re-styled into soft waves, her pale cheeks prettily flushed. To Karen's amazement she kissed her and said, 'Oh, it's so lovely to be back. Give me England every time.'

Ben was fine, she said, in reply to Karen's enquiry. They'd had a good and uneventful flight and she had taken him straight to her own little house so that she could look after him. 'He can't very well do for himself yet, and anyway it would be so silly for both of us to be lonely on our own, wouldn't it?' she said, flushing a little deeper.

'Very silly,' Karen agreed. Ben had a new nanny now, she thought, and felt mean for thinking it. That reminded her of Saul too, and she was trying so hard not to think of him every minute of every day, and most of the nights too, when she couldn't sleep.

She couldn't eat much, either. Perhaps it was true, perhaps you did pine away and die of love, like the heroines in the Victorian novels. You laughed at all that for sentimental sob-stuff until you had lost the man you loved, and then it didn't seem funny at all.

Jean returned to the workroom, taking charge of the women there with an authority and self-confidence she hadn't had before, discussing with Charlie and James Ward the various ways of enlisting and training new staff. Karen felt as if her own particular function in the company were gradually being whittled away, chip by chip. After a week she found one day that there was nothing at all for her to do. It happened to be on that particular day that Jean said, a little shyly, 'Would you like to come and have supper with us this evening, Karen? Ben would like to talk to you about the future of the company; he knows you're interested.'

The invitation was so unexpected that Karen didn't have time to think up an excuse. And anyway, she had promised Ben that they would still be friends, so the sooner they all got over the first slight awkwardness the better.

The evening wasn't as awkward as she had feared. The three of them slipped into their new roles with such ease that Karen realised straight away that this was how it was meant to be, and that she wouldn't have been nearly as 'right' for Ben as Jean was going to be. Jean's little house was spotless, the supper of chicken casserole followed by baked custard ('Ben still has to be a bit careful what he eats') was nicely cooked and daintily served. But most important of all, Jean was in love with Ben; it showed in every look, every word. It shone out of her like a radiance.

The talk was all of the new Clark's Components. 'I had a long letter from Japan this morning, from Saul,' Ben said, 'sending me on a copy of a report he has been working on while he's been out there. He's full of ideas for us, and it's all pretty thrilling. Can you believe, Karen, I'll have my own research lab, all properly fitted out. And I'll have a capable assistant ready to hand.' He grinned at Jean and she suddenly looked flustered and said she'd go and make some tea.

When they were alone, Karen said quietly, 'It's all coming good for you, isn't it Ben? I'm so glad.'

For a moment, looking into her eyes, his own eyes were clouded. Then he smiled. 'It'll take a little time, Karen, but—yes—it'll work out in the end. But what about your plans—have you made any? Saul mentioned something tentative about your going to London. Have you considered that?'

Karen shook her head. 'No, that's definitely out, it doesn't appeal in the least. I shall stay at home for a short time and help my father, and then I think I'd like to take some further training—in something—I haven't really thought much about it yet. I'll be packing up my things at the office on Friday, there's really nothing for me to do there now. I've told Mr Ward.'

Ben nodded, his forehead creasing in a troubled frown. 'I suppose that's best. But you know, Karen, I feel that somehow or other you're the one who's lost out on all that's happened. I feel bad about it.'

'You mustn't,' she said. 'I'll be O.K. I'm pretty good at bouncing back.'

'You're a wonderful girl, as I've always known,' Ben said softly. 'I wish——'

But Karen wasn't to know what he wished, for Jean came back with the tea then. And very soon afterwards Karen left. She had a feeling that next time she visited the little house Ben and Jean would be married. She sat in her car for a moment in the dark road looking back at the windows of the house, the lights shining from inside through the flowery curtains. It looked cosy and homelike and the heavy lump inside Karen's chest suddenly became an unbearable aching pain. She started the Mini's engine with a roar and drove for miles away from the town, until she was sure that both her parents would be occupied—her mother with her evening clinic at the hospital, her father with his surgery. Only then did she turn the car and drive back, to crawl up unnoticed to her room and lie dry-eyed and heavy-limbed on her bed.

It'll take a little time—that's what Ben had said. What Karen was afraid of was that it would take the rest of her life.

Friday was a dismal day. A thaw had set in and everywhere was grey and slushy. Even the usually cheerful spirits of the girls in the workroom seemed to be dampened by the weather. Karen spent the day sorting and packing things in the office, cleaning out drawers and cupboards, going over a few final points with James Ward. Then she did a tour of the workroom, saying goodbye to everyone. By now the staff knew more or less what was going to happen and they had been reassured that their jobs were safe. But they were unsettled by the idea of change, and dismayed that Karen would be leaving. One or two of the older ones voiced their indignation to her.

'I think it's a proper shame,' said Mrs Grayson, and the two girls at the adjoining work-benches nodded vehemently. 'You oughtn't to be losing your job, Miss Lane, just because we're being took over by some high and mighty big-wig.'

'It isn't like that really,' Karen told her, but Mrs Grayson looked sceptically at Karen's pale cheeks and heavy eyes and drew her own conclusions, which, as it happened, weren't far off the mark.

Karen had tea with Charlie and Jean at the afternoon tea-break, promised to look in and see them when everything was going full steam ahead once more, and took her coat down from the rack in the outside office for the last time. The funereal feeling had really struck now; she felt cold and numb as she shook hands with James Ward and went out to the car-park.

The sky had been getting darker all day, and now a curtain of cold rain met her as she opened the door. She lowered her head and groped her way towards her Mini.

A large form was approaching her, indistinct in the bad light. As she reached forward to put her key in the lock her hand was grabbed, held. She gave a gasp, peered upwards, and then her heart nearly stopped.

'Saul,' she croaked, 'what are you doing here?' And that was silly, because the whole place belonged to him now. 'I thought you were in Japan,' she added weakly.

'I was,' said Saul, and the sound of his voice cracked the ice inside her, moving through her veins like potent wine. 'And now I'm here, and so are you. I've been waiting for hours for you to appear. Come along, I want to talk to you.'

She saw the Rolls then, pulled up at the far end of the car-park. His arm was round her, urging her towards it and her feet followed helplessly where he led. In a kind of dream she found herself sitting in the passenger seat with Saul beside her, driving out of the town. She ceased to think or wonder, just sat there while weak fat tears ran slowly down her cheeks.

Once outside the town Saul pulled the car into a field-gate gap and switched off the engine. Outside the rain was heavier, beating against the windscreen. For a moment neither of them said a word, then Karen gave a great sob and thrust her fist against her mouth.

Saul's arms were round her and he was kissing her

urgently, almost angrily, and she could taste the salt of her tears as the old magic took hold and she began to kiss him back in a frenzied passion of love and longing.

'Let's get in the back,' he muttered, and before she knew what was happening he was pushing the door open. There was a moment's shock of cold as the rain struck, and then they were both sinking deep into cushiony comfort, arms entwined, their hearts beating against each other in a frenzy of desire.

'God, I've been crazy for you,' Saul muttered as he pulled off her jacket. His hands moved over her beneath the soft mohair of her top, moulding her breasts while his mouth fastened on hers, his lips, his tongue, probing, demanding. Then he moved away, wrenching at his own clothing until somehow, at last, they were locked together, flesh on flesh, hungry for each other, both of them satisfying their need greedily, with a compulsion that drove them with an urge that was as old as life itself.

At last it was over and they were still, the wild throb of their hearts quietening. Gently, Saul disentangled himself. 'You mustn't get cold, my darling.' He reached behind him to the parcel-shelf for a soft rug.

'Cold!' She giggled feebly. 'You're joking.'

'I refuse to let you die of pneumonia before I have a chance of showing you how much better it will be in proper surroundings. I just couldn't wait, that's my excuse.'

'Neither could I,' Karen said, very low. 'You make me shameless.'

His laugh had a note of triumph. 'That was the idea—a surprise attack before you had the chance to think up some act to put me off.'

'Now look——' She began to sit up but he pushed her back.

'Later,' he said in his old peremptory tone. 'Just now we need civilisation and warmth, where do you suggest we go? Where were you off to when I kidnapped you?'

'I was going home,' she said.

'Home. Now that's a good word. May I come too?'

Karen began to pull down her mohair top and fasten up her jacket. One of the buttons was hanging off. She pushed back her tangle of hair, and said, 'I'll have to creep in the back way if we do.' She leaned forward and peered at the illuminated clock on the dashboard. 'Wait a minute though—with any luck my parents will both still be out, we might just manage to tidy ourselves up before we're discovered.'

'Good, we'll risk it then. I'm tired of hotels. You stay where you are and keep warm. I'll drive to your home if you'll direct me. He got back into the front seat. 'Are your parents broadminded?' he enquired.

'Tolerably,' she told him as he started the engine and turned the car round. 'But they might draw the line at their only daughter behaving disgracefully with a man they've never seen before.'

Saul applied the brakes momentarily and said over his shoulder. 'Not even if they were destined to see a great deal of him in the future? Not even if he was the man that the said only daughter was going to marry?'

Karen flopped back speechless as he drove the big car into the town at an alarming rate.

'Of course we can put you up, Saul. We wouldn't hear of your going to a hotel.' Karen's mother turned a smile of approval and satisfaction upon her prospective son-in-law. 'The bed in the spare room is made up already, Karen. Run up and put a couple of hot-water bottles in.'

Karen flew upstairs. Her feet, which had been so leaden, now seemed to have wings—like Puck—or was it Ariel?—who put a girdle round the earth in forty minutes.

She turned on the hot tap in the bathroom. Daddy and Mother really were rather marvellous. If they had been surprised, when they walked in, to find their daughter in the arms of a perfect stranger on the living-room sofa, they had taken it all in their stride. They had shown their customary calm, and Saul had behaved beautifully. As she tucked the hot-water bottles into the spare room bed she gave the duvet a little pat. I'll be with you again soon, my love, she whispered. But not tonight.

By the time supper was over Saul might have been an old friend of the family. And when, finally, the doctor and his wife retired tactfully to the study to hold what Doctor Lane smilingly called a 'medical conference' Saul pulled Karen down beside him on to the sofa, in front of a crackling log fire, and wrapped his arms round her, saying, 'I like your parents.'

'I'm glad,' she said. 'They like you.'

He looked genuinely pleased. 'Do they? How can you be sure?'

'Oh, I can be sure,' she said. 'You've no idea how politely crushing they could have been if they hadn't.'

'Well, certainly your father didn't demur too much when I asked him for his daughter's hand in marriage, when you and your mother were out preparing the supper,' he smiled. 'How delightfully old-fashioned that sounds.'

'And Mummy is already planning the wedding reception,' Karen said. 'She says she can take a fortnight's holiday from her clinic in July.'

'*July?*' Saul broke in, horrified. 'I can't wait that long. Only long enough for you to meet my folk and break the good news to them.'

'I hope they like me.' She was suddenly nervous of meeting the people who had given so much to Saul, who loved him so deeply.

'They will,' he said confidently. 'They'll be delighted with you. As I am.' He bent his head and began to nuzzle her neck gently.

She pulled away. 'Behave yourself, Mr Marston,' she said primly. 'Or you know what's likely to happen.'

He sighed. 'You're right. I mustn't take advantage of your parents' enlightened good nature.' He sat up and moved away along the sofa. 'O.K. we'll talk instead. I want an explanation from you, woman.'

'Explanation?' she murmured dreamily.

'Yes indeed. What was the idea of that big act you put on after the dinner on our last night in Acapulco? It had me fooled for a while, I must admit, I really believed that you were going to marry Ben Clark—that you'd been rooting for him all the time, even when you were in my bed. I went through the blackest of black hells that night, and the whole time I was in Japan, trying to persuade myself that I could get used to seeing you married to Ben. When I got back from Tokyo yesterday I came straight up here and went to Ben's home address, but he wasn't there. I found out from a neighbour that he was staying with his fiancée and she gave me the address. It took every bit of my courage to ring that bell, expecting that you would answer the door. When some other girl did I nearly burst into tears and kissed her, because it wasn't you.'

'It was Jean,' Karen said. 'Jean McBride. I think they're going to get married.'

'Well, good luck to them. But you still haven't come up with the explanation.'

Karen looked away, biting her lip. Everything was so perfect now, she didn't want to explain, to seem to accuse. She wanted to forget the whole episode, to wipe it out as if it had never happened.

But he was waiting and there was no getting out of it.

'I suppose it was my sticky pride,' she said at last. 'But it hurt when I knew you had been—been using me.'

He sat up. 'You knew *what*? Good God, girl, you'll have to control that imagination of yours.'

She glared at him. 'Imagination? It wasn't imagination. What was I supposed to think when I met Liz Walker going into your bedroom—dressed in nothing but a nylon wrap—and *that* was hanging open! When she was kind enough to inform me that you were expecting her and that my services as a smoke-screen wouldn't be required any longer? When she went into your room and shut the door in my face? Oh no . . .' her voice rose three tones '. . . imagination didn't come into it.'

Saul was looking sterner than she had ever seen him look. 'You believed her? You believed that I was the kind of man who could behave like that—after what you and I had had together the night before?' His voice was icy cold, he was miles away from her.

Karen's world began to rock horribly. He was looking at her as if—as if he hated her. She had lost him. Oh, why couldn't she have just shut up and said nothing?

Desolately she lifted swimming eyes to his. 'How could I not believe? I went back into my bedroom and—and I heard you laughing together. And I guessed you must be laughing at me. And then——'

she bit her lip hard '—then the laughing stopped and there was just—silence. I knew what was happening and—and I couldn't take it. I ran away down the stairs—out into the fresh air——'

She sat shivering, waiting for him to say something, waiting for him to say that he'd made a mistake when he asked her to marry him, that he didn't want a suspicious wife who spied on him and listened through bedroom walls.

'It doesn't matter now——' she whispered through her tears.

'Of course it matters,' he burst out angrily. Then, to her amazement, he reached out and gathered her into his arms with great tenderness. 'Oh, my little love,' he said. 'I wouldn't have hurt you for the world. That bloody wench, Liz Walker—I'd like to wring her lovely white neck for her.'

'Then—then you weren't expecting her?'

'Of course I wasn't. What there was between us had finished months ago—before she married Harry. But she wouldn't give up, she wouldn't let herself believe it was over, in spite of some straight talking on my part. I was furious when she walked into my room that afternoon—especially so since I'd escaped early to be with you. I wanted to get rid of her quickly but it wasn't so easy. I tried laughing her out of it but that didn't work, so I shut up. The silence you heard must have been when she went into her seduction routine— and I'll leave you to guess how that went. I had to take evasive action and in the end I pushed her out bodily. If you'd hung around a bit longer you might have witnessed the eviction,' he finished grimly.

Karen thought for a time in silence. Then she said, 'So you did really want me to come with you to Acapulco?'

He looked puzzled for a moment, then he said,

'Now look, let's get this straight now and then we needn't think about it again. What, exactly, did that busy little imagination of yours work out when you put on that great hard-boiled act for me on the night of the dinner?'

Karen twisted her hands together in silence, trying to get her thoughts straight, which wasn't easy when Saul's arm was holding her close and his head was pressed against her hair.

At last she said slowly, 'After what Liz Walker told me—after I'd had time to think about it—I remembered how you'd made such a point of my coming to Mexico with Ben, and that you seemed to be going out of your way to demonstrate to everyone—including Harry Walker—that I was your current girl-friend. I thought you looked on me as simple and unsophisticated and believed I would be easy to manipulate. It all seemed to hang together.'

'Even that night you spent in my arms?' he said quietly. 'Even when I told you I loved you? You thought that was all a put-up job?'

She hung her head. 'I decided that it probably hadn't meant very much to you. You must have had lots of girls.'

'Lots,' he agreed. 'I've forgotten most of their names. Now, if you've finished your little scenario I'll tell you exactly what actually *did* happen. Let's go back to that first day when I walked into Clark's office and saw you there, looking so cool and tempting in your white blouse and your red skirt, with your hair all neat and silky and your beautiful eyes weighing me up so coolly.'

'You remember what I was wearing?'

'Down to the toes of your boots,' he smiled, and went on, 'I suppose what's given me some success in business is a certain flair for recognising what I want when I see it, and making decisions promptly. Well, I wanted you that morning, and I determined to get you. Oh, I fancied you, of course I did, you're a beautiful girl, Karen. But there was something more than that— something that was new to me. Call it love at first sight if you like. Everything slotted into place and I knew you were the girl I wanted for good—the problem was how I was going to go about getting you. I'd have liked to take you in my arms then and there. What would you have said if I had?' He pushed her hair aside and kissed her softly behind her ear.

She snuggled closer. 'I'd have thought you were bonkers and asked Charlie to see you out.'

'Precisely. So I had to proceed with caution—which is what I thought I'd been doing. Why do you think I insisted on your coming with Ben to Mexico? Why did I ask you straight away if you were going to marry him? Why did I spend every spare minute I had with you? I was doing my damnest to make you want me. I thought if we fancied each other then you might really fall in love with me afterwards. I was so sure of success, I nearly messed up everything with my bloody self-confidence. Many years ago I talked myself into believing I couldn't fail in anything—but there's always a first time, and until yesterday I thought failure had hit me at last.'

She reached up and stroked his hair. 'I wouldn't want to marry a loser,' she said.

He caught her hand and turned it over, kissing the palm tenderly and when she looked up there was such a fire of love in his eyes that she felt she was melting in the flame of it.

'A first time for everything,' he mused. 'You seem to provide first times for me. The first time I've made love in the back of a car. The first time I've told a girl I love her and really meant it with every fibre of me.

The first time I've thought of marriage with certainty and trust and faith. We'll have a good marriage, my love, I swear it. Can it be soon—long before next July? *Please*.'

She began to laugh as she held up her mouth for his kiss. 'You always get what you want in the end, don't you? Why should this be any different?'

Coming Next Month

879 THAI TRIANGLE Jayne Bauling
In Thailand an artist tries to bring two brothers together before it's too late. In love with one, she can't break her promise to the other—not even to avoid heartache.

880 PILLOW PORTRAITS Rosemary Carter
An assignment to ghostwrite a famous artist's autobiography seems like the chance of a lifetime—until he insists on her baring her soul, too, even her deepest secret.

881 DARK DREAM Daphne Clair
When her childhood sweetheart brings home a fiancée, a young woman finds herself marrying a widower who claims to love her. Yet he still dreams about his first wife!

882 POINT OF IMPACT Emma Darcy
On a ferry in Sydney Harbour it is a night to celebrate. Although the man she once loved is present, a model throws caution to the wind and announces her engagement. The shockwaves are immediate!

883 INJURED INNOCENT Penny Jordan
Co-guardians are at loggerheads—not so much over their differing views on how to raise the little girls as over an unresolved conflict from the past.

884 DANGER ZONE Madeleine Ker
An English fashion designer in New York is drawn to a successful merchant banker, despite his disturbing, reckless streak and the strain it places on their love.

885 SWEET AS MY REVENGE Susan Napier
The owner of an Australian secretarial agency is trapped and forced to face the consequences of her foolhardy act to save her brother's career. But no one tricks her into falling in love.

886 ICE INTO FIRE Lilian Peake
When her parents' marriage shatters, a young woman vows never to be burned by love. But at a Swiss chalet, a man who equally mistrusts emotion manages to melt her resolve.

Available in May wherever paperback books are sold, or through Harlequin Reader Service.

In the U.S.
P.O. Box 1397
Buffalo, N.Y.
14240-1397

In Canada
P.O. Box 2800, Postal Station A
5170 Yonge Street
Willowdale, Ontario M2N 6J3

No one Can Resist . . .

HARLEQUIN REGENCY ROMANCES

Regency romances take you back to a time when men fought for their ladies' honor and passions—a time when heroines had to choose between love and duty . . . with love always the winner!

Enjoy these three authentic novels of love and romance set in one of the most colorful periods of England's history.

Lady Alicia's Secret by Rachel Cosgrove Payes

She had to keep her true identity hidden—at least until she was convinced of his love!

Deception So Agreeable by Mary Butler

She reacted with outrage to his false proposal of marriage, then nearly regretted her decision.

The Country Gentleman by Dinah Dean

She refused to believe the rumors about him—certainly until they could be confirmed or denied!

Everyone Loves . . .

HARLEQUIN GOTHIC ROMANCES

A young woman lured to an isolated estate far from help and civilization . . . a man, lonely, tortured by a centuries' old commitment . . . and a sinister force threatening them both and their newfound love . . . Read these three superb novels of romance and suspense . . . as timeless as love and as filled with the unexpected as tomorrow!

Return To Shadow Creek by Helen B. Hicks

She returned to the place of her birth—only to discover a sinister plot lurking in wait for her. . . .

Shadows Over Briarcliff by Marilyn Ross

Her visit vividly brought back the unhappy past—and with it an unknown evil presence. . . .

The Blue House by Dolores Holliday

She had no control over the evil forces that were driving her to the brink of madness. . . .

WORLDWIDE LIBRARY IS YOUR TICKET TO ROMANCE, ADVENTURE AND EXCITEMENT

Experience it all in these big, bold Bestsellers— Yours exclusively from WORLDWIDE LIBRARY WHILE QUANTITIES LAST

To receive these Bestsellers, complete the order form, detach and send together with your check or money order (include 75¢ postage and handling), payable to WORLDWIDE LIBRARY, to:

In the U.S.	In Canada
WORLDWIDE LIBRARY	WORLDWIDE LIBRARY
901 Fuhrmann Blvd.	P.O. Box 2800, 5170 Yonge Street
Buffalo, N.Y. 14269	Postal Station A, Willowdale, Ontario M2N 6J3

Quant.	Title	Price
_____	**WILD CONCERTO**, Anne Mather	$2.95
_____	**A VIOLATION**, Charlotte Lamb	$3.50
_____	**SECRETS**, Sheila Holland	$3.50
_____	**SWEET MEMORIES**, LaVyrle Spencer	$3.50
_____	**FLORA**, Anne Weale	$3.50
_____	**SUMMER'S AWAKENING**, Anne Weale	$3.50
_____	**FINGER PRINTS**, Barbara Delinsky	$3.50
_____	**DREAMWEAVER**, Felicia Gallant/Rebecca Flanders	$3.50
_____	**EYE OF THE STORM**, Maura Seger	$3.50
_____	**HIDDEN IN THE FLAME**, Anne Mather	$3.50
_____	**ECHO OF THUNDER**, Maura Seger	$3.95
_____	**DREAM OF DARKNESS**, Jocelyn Haley	$3.95
	YOUR ORDER TOTAL	$_____
	New York and Arizona residents add appropriate sales tax	$_____
	Postage and Handling	$ .75
	I enclose	$_____

NAME _____

ADDRESS _____ APT.# _____

CITY _____

STATE/PROV. _____ ZIP/POSTAL CODE _____

WW-1-3

What the press says about Harlequin romance fiction...

"When it comes to romantic novels...
Harlequin is the indisputable king."
— *New York Times*

"...always with an upbeat, happy ending."
— *San Francisco Chronicle*

"Women have come to trust these
stories about contemporary people,
set in exciting foreign places."
— *Best Sellers*, New York

"The most popular reading matter of
American women today."
— *Detroit News*

"...a work of art."
— *Globe & Mail*, Toronto

Take 4 novels and a surprise gift FREE